We Shall Sing a Song into the Deep

WE SHALL SING A SONG INTO THE DEEP

ANDREW KELLY STEWART

A TOM DOHERTY ASSOCIATES BOOK

NEW YORK

WE SHALL SING A SONG INTO THE DEEP

Copyright © 2021 by Andrew Kelly Stewart

Cover photographs © Getty Images
Cover design by Christine Foltzer

Edited by Diana M. Pho

A Tordotcom Book
Published by Tom Doherty Associates
120 Broadway
New York, NY 10271

www.tor.com

Tor® is a registered trademark of Macmillan Publishing Group, LLC.

ISBN 978-1-250-79090-3 (ebook)
ISBN 978-1-250-79087-3 (trade paperback)

First Edition: March 2021

We Shall Sing a Song into the Deep

1

THE PEAL RESOUNDS through the boat, through the frame of my bunk. I feel it in my jaw, my teeth. Reverberation.

And again.

Brother Silas, knocking the rusty-headed mallet against the hull.

The boat is a bell.

Three deep, resonating tolls. *Thong. Thong* and *thong.* Waver and fade.

Call to Matins. The Night Office.

The compartment pitches downward. Weight shifts. Cold toes tingle, alive. The deepest dive of the day. One hundred fathoms.

Bodies turn, roused from first sleep. Old metal springs *plink.* Sleepy shapes roll languidly from their bunks. I know them all, even in the dimness. Lazlo, lean and short, but strong. Caleb, mousy and frail. St. John with his large knobby head, and tall, soft-padding Ephraim. Stifled coughs. No talking. Silence is observed. Must be.

I follow, though my belly aches to move. More than hunger, I worry, for I know those pangs as I know my hands. Something else. A two-day malady thus far. But I move, climb down from my bunk, stacked third highest. My toes know their purchase. Salt-corroded frames. Grit-grated deck. We don our gunnysack robes in this perennial dusk.

One sculpin-oil lamp hangs at a tilt from the forward berthing bulkhead. Fat-gummed glass. Sputter and fishy reek. In a line, we work our way aft, up the main corridor at a slant.

No speaking. But we will sing, yes.

I commence warming up our voices. My ear tells my throat how to find the key. I always find it. This is one of the reasons why I'm the Cantor. The anchoring line. With pitch rooted, the other voices meet it. Step up, step down. Two steps up, two steps down, and back to the middle.

Our collective hum joins the unending chorus of loud pinging, knocking, clanging.

These sounds aren't coming from Brother Silas's hammer, nor the submarine's many machines, which sing their own unending chorus as they work to keep us alive, keep the boat moving.

This is pressure. The weight of the dark sea squeezing the old welds and joints and seals, against valves and piping.

Our vessel, the *Leviathan*.

Its crew, the last of the penitent men on this wicked, ruined earth.

We scale aft through the mess, through the galley. No victuals. Not until later. Hunger reminds us. Of where we came from, that poisoned, wicked world above. Of our salvation.

Up, past missile control and the radio room, we join the exodus of brothers leaving their stations, follow them through the hatchway, ducking, descending corroded ladders until, at last, we gather in the missile compartment.

Our chapel.

The largest single space on the *Leviathan*. We file down to the lower deck, between the bases of the great red columns. Sixteen of them. Eight spaced parallel on either side. Each is forty feet tall, reaching from the lowest recesses of the boat to the top deck. Each is wide. Like the pillars I've imagined, reading the Book of Judges, of Samson, and how, though his hair was shorn from his head by the betrayer, and though he was powerless and blinded, he still toppled the temple of Dagon.

They once held His fire, these pillars. Each one. And, when He spoke, Caplain listened. Unleashed each. Those first days of tribulation.

One remains.

One missile.

The Last Judgment.

The chamber, the whole vessel, levels. A litany of bright, high rings toll from the brass bell hanging on the main level above. We are at depth. One hundred fathoms.

Almost all attend the office. We Choristers, our fellow brothers, the eight elders. The crew of the *Leviathan*. Those manning the helm, the watch, the radar are exempt. Otherwise, when the bell tolls, you abandon your duties, whatever they may be, and there are many: working the bilge pumps, harvesting the mushrooms from the evaporators, mending the nets, pulling in the nets and culling the haul, sick fish from the good fish—less good fish these days—rendering the fats for unguent and fuel, cleaning the battery terminals, draining away the corrosive acid, monitoring the oxygen generator, the CO_2 levels, and, of course, tending the heart of this beast, the reactor, which always requires a watchful eye, pressure and heat contained in mere piping, poison behind it all. God's light.

Those who tend the reactor—the Forgotten—do not come forward for prayers or song either. They are not seen again once they are sent back through the tunnel. They serve their purpose, those forsaken.

And we serve ours. We Choristers. The five of us who remain. Who have not succumbed to sickness. Whose voices have not broken. Whose voices still reach the highest, loftiest of ranges.

We sing. Lift the hearts of our brothers.

We find God. We call out to him from these depths, and he answers.

Spoonful of rancid oil. Choke it down.

For our throats. These divine instruments.

Elders—most bent, mottled skin, toothless—stand forward, but the younger, broader-backed brothers space themselves along the walls, between and behind the pillars, against the machinery, against the electronic consoles that are dead and scavenged for parts long ago.

We Choristers, we the young, we the ones cut in order to preserve pure voice, gather in the narrow cella. Before dais and altar and psalter.

Caplain Amita normally leads Matins—Caplain with his stooped frame, his round chin, his eyes that always seem to be closed, even when they are open—but he has been absent this past week. Ill. His skin was a yellow grey last I saw him—scant more illumination here, in the chapel. Skin thin as Bible pages. Limbs turned inward. Stiff, like the already-dead.

Ex-Oh Marston officiates today, steps up to the dais.

Tall. Too tall for a submariner, some have said of him, which seems to be a truth. Has a hunch, for all the years of ducking through hatches. Of the original crew, decades ago. Head shorn, like all of us. Pate speckled like an egg. I've seen speck-led eggs once. Blues and pinks and browns. Dented, his. Face gaunt, gaunt. Scared by some battle done or some ill deed done to him. Look of driftwood.

Merciless with the strop, Ex-Oh.

Especially when it comes to the Choristers.

We deserve it.

We come from wickedness, from Topside. Rescued. Given purpose. A chance to redeem our souls. We aren't the only ones who have been saved—there are those brothers who were taken aboard as children who could not sing but were strong, able, and needed to serve on the crew.

Like us, they had to earn their place. Many have gone on to take the vows of the Brotherhood. Brother Silas. Brother Callum.

But many have not.

There cannot be any question of faith.

No faltering in our resolve.

We must be ready for the day. For it is coming. And coming soon. That is what Ex-Oh says. What Caplain says.

And when the end has finally come, and He has deemed the days of tribulation done, we will launch His Last Judgment. And then we shall journey to the very bottom of the great abyss. To the lowest fathom. And we shall sing a song into that deep, on that last day, and the sea shall finally give up her dead. And we, with them, shall ascend into the light. As below, so above!

A raised, slender, yellow-nailed hand brings all to order.

"*Deus, in adiutorium meum intende,*" Ex-Oh intones, thin nose angled up to the deck. Flat. Reverent. Monotonous.

"*Domine, ad adiumandun me fastina,*" we respond in equal monotony.

This vessel, this *Leviathan,* often so hollow, is full now. Brimming with voice. Sound pressing against the hull, fighting against the darkness that presses in.

Doxology follows. This, sung in a mode that hugs one primary note and strays little from it: "*Gloria Patri, et Filio, et Spiritui Sancto.*"

I know some of these words. *Glory to the father, the son, the holy spirit.* Caplain has taught me some Latin. An old language. The language of the Church. Has let me know them and keep them for myself. The others sing by memory. Words and notes, unpinned to page or history. I've told Lazlo I know some of these words. It seems wrong that we don't understand the meaning of what we sing.

The psalter, big as a crouching boy, bound in shark hide, lay opened, hymn selected. "The Heart of the Leviathan." One I need not squint to see by, penned in violet squid ink.

"*Azure, bla-zing heart. O, keep us true. Your spark, in the bel-ly of the Le-vi-a-th-an.*"

Melody, at last. Harmony.

As Cantor, as principal, I take the descant. My melody floats above the others. Flies.

Singing is the only time my heart does not feel burdened. When I feel God. I think it is not vanity to sing. To like the sound of my voice. Higher than the others. Like light, bouncing off every bulkhead, reaching out over every surface of the concave metal hull.

Some of us Choristers change, even after the cutting. Those with the broken voices, Demis—those who can no longer sing—are sent aft with the rest of those taken from Topside and deemed unworthy. Through the tunnel, forced to work in the engine room, the reactor chamber, with the blue poison and fume. They are beyond our sight. Beyond His grace. Not to be spoken of. Not to be prayed for. They came from the world above, like us—like me. But God did not spare them. They are the Forgotten.

I have heard of their fate. Grease smear and boils and steam burn and bloody hacking. And poison from the reactor. Lazlo has seen them. Has smelled them.

A smell like everything is wrong.

Scripture now, this in the common tongue, for all to comprehend.

"To the roots of the mountains I sank down," Ex-Oh reads from the book, voice like a hatch squealing on its rusty hinges. Feel the words in my spine. *"The earth 'neath barred me in forever. But you, LORD my God, brought my life up from the pit."*

Book of Jonah.

"As below, so above!" Ex-Oh calls out.

And this congregation answers in refrain.

"Remy," Lazlo whispers into my ear, once we have filed out, dispersed to our duties, once we are distanced from the ears of elders. He speaks differently than the rest. His words have a lilt to them. His skin darker, despite being kept from the sun for so many years. Eight years.

"Your scar must be bleeding," he says, pointing down.

I stop, lift my foot.

A drop of blood spots my big toe. Dusky red. Blackish.

Scars do still bleed. Even years later, they can reopen and weep.

But this wouldn't be true for me.

Not a cut or scrape, either.

My heart crashes into my stomach.

It's happened.

————————

The first meal of the day is always the same.

Broth of bladderwrack. Dried mushroom and algae cake. "Grey cake," Lazlo calls it. We grow and harvest the mushrooms from atop the generators. Used to be a time we would have fish press as well, but now press comes at the meal following Vespers. If we're lucky. With our slurry and drip.

Brackish draught.

These meals provide little lasting sustenance.

There has been no raid above for some time. No meal or flour or canned, sweet things. Not that I would have an appetite for such delicacies.

Lazlo is trying to speak with me, from across the table.

We are free to speak in the mess. In whispers, but it's allowed. A low chatter amongst the four tables, like steam.

Today, I have few words.

Lazlo wonders why, I know. Muddied eyes, squinted. Little body hunched. Big, red cheeks. Scurvy efflorescence, Brother Karson calls it. From a lack of fresh victuals. We all suffer it. I taste blood at the back of my throat when I wake. Bleeding, raw gums.

Worst is when the old scars open again.

Lazlo asks again if I am in pain, that he can get me a poultice if needed. Poultices help with the swelling, with the bleeding. He's close with Brother Ignacio, in the galley.

I tell him it's nothing, though my throat is tight with unsaid truths.

Caleb, the youngest, and the one with the freshest scar, has endured the worst of the pain and the bleeding. So much that when we have steamed sargassum or kelp, I give him some of my portion—one of the few plants from the sea that can stave off the scurvy.

Today, he looks pale.

"You know, if you bleed too much before your twelfth birthday, you're in greater danger of turning out a Demi," St. John says, in that stiff way he says things. Speaks the same way he sits—straight, rigid. Face tight with superiority.

Caleb, already pale, goes fully white.

"And you know where Demis go . . ." St. John says, leaning in, a taunting smirk. He is not above plain meanness, St. John. A long nose. A bulbous head prone to shaving rash. We all must keep our hair shorn, of course. Honed shells do the work well enough. In skilled hands, anyway.

"Don't scare him," Ephraim, the eldest of us, chimes in, unamused. "That isn't true, Caleb."

Caleb takes in a bracing breath and returns to his meal; all the while, St. John continues to wear a prideful smirk.

If voices break after a cutting, it occurs by the age of twelve or thirteen. Caused by an unblessed blade, they say, but Brother Silas has told me privately that it sometimes just happens. There's no accounting for it.

St. John has passed that age where the breaking of a voice happens. Fourteen years. He has been vicious and haughty ever since. The truth is that half of all those castrated have either died from their wounds or turned. Become Demis, and must be purified in other ways.

I know that St. John has been waiting for my voice to break, or Lazlo's, so that he might ascend to our positions. I know

I will never change. But Lazlo is still in that dangerous range where, at any day, his voice just might leave him.

Any Chorister's greatest fear.

Like God's wrath, the reactor must be appeased—must be tended, or it will consume us as well. Brother Calvert explained it better to me—that the heart of the *Leviathan*, when functioning properly, can provide energy for decades. Energy that powers the turbines which turn the screw, which powers the oxygen generators and water desalinators, and runs the fans and all the electrics—but like everything else, it is failing. The reactor is powerful, but its power is poisonous. Some invisible poison called radiation. And yet, people must go into the reactor room in order to moderate the power. To keep it from overheating.

This is the work that purifies the Forgotten.

"I only mean that Caleb would be right to worry," St. John continues. "And Lazlo."

I grasp Lazlo's hand to keep him from responding.

I see Ephraim's patience has thinned as well. He's about to respond when the Ex-Oh enters the mess—ducks to clear the hatch. Choristers and brothers fall silent. A rare appearance. Normally, he and the other elders eat their meals in the officers' wardroom. Mouth bent down. Thin eyebrows raised. Eyes squinting and small. The dimness has made most of the elders near blind. Grey and dead-looking, like the eyes of the odd fish we sometimes catch in our nets, the ones that come from the darkest depths of the sea. Always surveying, scouring us for impropriety. For sin.

He levels his gaze upon me. I fight the urge to shrink.

My stomach twists into a reef knot.

"Come." He ushers me with his yellow fingers. "Caplain

wishes to have a word."

Lazlo's ash eyes flash downward. Fear of the Ex-Oh? Of what such a meeting might mean? It has been some time since I have been summoned to his quarters.

There is no mistaking St. John's expression—a simmering jealousy.

The caplain's quarters are forward, on the same deck as the control room, past dials and blinking panels and tables full of water-stained charts and periscope tubes and the helm and sonar room. We are only allowed to enter this area upon permission.

"Do not tax him needlessly," Ex-Oh warns, leaning over me. "He is very ill."

About his neck hangs a piece of metal, bent, chipped to look like a key.

We wear keys. Mine, dried kelp, shaped into eye and stem and teeth, held by a length of old electric wire.

"Aye, Ex-Oh."

"And you will report to me anything of import he might share with you, yes?"

I nod. He sees my hesitation, peers down at me a moment longer before taking his leave.

I rap once and hear, on the other side of the soft wooden door, a weak, raspy invitation to enter.

The caplain's cabin is the largest of the personal quarters on board. Even so, this is no great space—most of it given over to desk and shelves of books—most of which I have read. *The Confessions of St. Augustine. The Rule of St. Bene-*

dict. The Letters of Jerome. But more than just religious texts. Books on sea life, on sailing. Navigation. Ancient history. Music. Even a few novels. About castaways and adventures and His will.

Caplain is tucked into his bunk. Stepping forward, I cross a fetid threshold. Not just the rank oil fueling the three lamps that illuminate the chamber—but a deeper, darker odor that lingers in the room heavy as grease smoke. Eel bile and bilge.

Sunk, deflated. Caplain's skin, a map of palm fruit–colored open sores. I hear his ragged breathing, even standing at two arms' distance.

"Come into the light, Cantor," he says, as though exhaling. The wheeze like the compressors make when kept running for too long.

A whalebone-and-thatch stool stands at the bedside. I sit. Close to him, very close.

His clouded eyes seek me out. They do not find me. His pale hand does. Fingers, long and pale and bony, like the legs of the white spiders that spin their webs in the corners of the balneary, folded together.

"I fished you out of the sea," he says, part of him in the past.

"Yes," I tell him. He has told me this before. I don't remember it. Not really. Perhaps the taste of salt and blood on my cracked lips. The sun-scoured feeling of my skin. Angry, raw. But sun.

Light.

And an illustrated image. Of a palm tree set against blue sea, rooted in yellow sand. Some piece of wavering cloth, a banner.

But the whiteness. The warmth. That is what has always lingered most.

"My little Moses," he says. A sound comes from him. Was it meant to be a laugh? A strangled one. "Plucked you from the ragged sea, from a sinking boat. From the wicked world. Couldn't have been more than five or six. But smart. Even then, I knew you were special. That voice. That's why . . . why I kept you. Despite it all. Why I have taught you.

"God told me. To keep you. And I did. I knew it was meant to be when I heard your voice. An angel's voice. We have kept quite some confidence, haven't we? You and I?" he asks, trying to muster energy for sitting up. He wears something like a grin. A gap-toothed, red-lipped smile. A black void of a maw.

How have we kept it secret so long?

Such tight quarters. Shared bunks and ablutions.

But we Choristers and brothers bathe in our linens. Thin, sopping cloth plastered to skin masks enough. And the darkness. In this darkness, one could hide almost anything.

"They'll soon find out about me," I blurt out, unable to keep it inside any longer, voice trembling. I don't want for him to see my fear. He, who knows me better than even Lazlo.

"Ah, so the curse has come to you," he says. His cold hand squeezes mine with a surprising strength. Quells the terror that has been twisting inside me since Matins.

We spoke some time ago about this eventuality. About how to handle it, if it happened.

"God will protect you, child. There was a time when I wondered," Caplain says, "would He see fit to stop all these—*female* processes of yours—when He saw that you had found a home amongst us? Among the last of the righteous. But I've gone off that thinking—His will remains cryptic as ever. Even to us, the penitent. Though what remains clear, even to a man who has lost his sight, is that God allowed you to be saved for a purpose. To wit, I have summoned you today." He winces, quite suddenly, a throe of pain or palsy. He, at last, breathes.

Then he lets go my hand. Has left something behind in my palm. A cold, thin object. In the oil light, a silvery key. Long, toothed.

"Caplain?" I ask, looking down at it.

"For the Last Judgment. It cannot be launched without it."

"But what of yours," I say, pointing. I see it lying there against pale skin, against a washboard rack of ribs.

"It was the old captain's habit to wear a false key—before the war. Before we heard God's word and took this submarine in His name. A secret he shared with me, our old captain."

Captain.

Such a strange variation on the word. A precursor to the holy position that all on board have come to know and revere.

"Such a small object that wields so much power must be protected. Hidden from even the most loyal. This key that I give to you—it is the real one. I have kept it hidden." Caplain pauses to swab his lips with a purple tongue.

"But . . . but why? Why this deception?"

The old man closes his eyes. "I've waited these long years—have built this order, have put our prayers and praises and psalms into the depths—where God may hear us. I have also been listening, yes. Waiting for His word that the years of tribulation have finally come to an end. I expected it after some seven years. Seven years after I answered that first call. Launched the missiles. We unleashed all the fury of heaven upon that wicked world above. Yet one did not launch. Divine intervention, I thought. Saved for later. For purpose. To usher in that final terrible judgment. I have been listening, but I have heard nothing"—and his foggy eyes are staring at nothing. "I listened, I listened," he breathes. "I have long promised that our final dive would . . . would come soon, that our long years of service would finally be rewarded. But I see now that my role in the grand plan shall soon be done. And I realize now that I have put my trust in an unfit heir to this Brotherhood."

I draw in a hot breath.

Have I heard it correctly? Never—*never*—has the caplain shared such notions. He's lost his mind, I think. I should stand. Should go. Remember him as I have always known him. Not this rambling man.

Caplain continues. "Ex-Oh Marston is a true disciple. A strict observer. Unfailing in his practice of devotion. A stern disciplinarian. But he will not hear the Word when the time comes. His own ego stands in the way of that. An artless soul. He will rely upon a flawed judgment as to when we should deliver the Last Judgment."

"And you think I will hear the word? I'm from Topside. From the wicked world—"

"And given unto us by Grace," Caplain interjects. "Purpose. As I said, you have *purpose*. We can't know it yet."

"What about Brother Silas, or Brother Ernesto . . . they are wise, they are good—"

"You, Cantor. It must be you."

"But . . ." I tread carefully here, key still in my hand, weighing cold. Heavy as an anchor. "If Ex-Oh does try to launch, he'll quickly discover the key is false."

"You will remain silent; you will keep the key hidden if you have not heard the call from God."

"He is a . . . fierce man," I say, cannot help but whisper. What if Ex-Oh is at the door, listening at this very moment? I lean in, wall of astringent liniment mingled with rot. "Won't he have guessed that you've given the real key to someone?"

"He will not expect it to be you," Caplain says, words weary now. Weighted like ballast. "You, he will expect the least. And God will protect you."

I think he might be near sleeping now, by the weakened draw of breath, the closed, swollen lids.

"But . . . what will that sound like?" I ask. "God's voice?"

"I heard . . ." he begins. Far away, again. Lost in memory. Eyes shut, as though the lids are too heavy to open. "The leviathans. Their song. Behind their song. A voice from the deep. You listen, Sister Remy. I know you do. I have seen you listening. For one to sing as you do, they must first know how to listen."

"And what if I listen and, as with you, I never hear His word?" I ask.

Caplain opens his bloody, blackened mouth, as though about to speak. But shakes his head. An idea, apparently, too worrisome. A thought that knits his grey, wispy brows. A specter of doubt? I know that shadow. Have felt it cross me. This, I have told no one. Not even Lazlo.

"You will know, Sister Remy," a rattling whisper. "You will know."

Head bowed, I feel a tear crawl its way hotly down my cheek, reach my dry lips. Salty burn. He will be gone soon, this man. Death has already ensnared his body, pulling him down into the darkness. This man who saved me, though I was a girl and should have been tossed into the sea. Who has taught me. Kept me hidden.

"As below, so above," I say, waiting for his refrain.

But it doesn't come. He has drifted off into some troubled reverie.

There is only the guttering of the oil flames. The incessant rattle-whir of a ventilation fan. Tinny smell. Sits on my tongue. The creaking of fathoms of water, pressing down upon us.

Ast ego te posthac oculisque animoque tenebo, aequor ubi in lucem funera rapta feret.

AT THE RINGING OF LAUDS, a group of four brothers bears Caplain Amita's remains into the chapel and rests his thin, clothbound, bonefish body upon the platform where we Choristers would normally stand.

"Lauds is the hour where we praise the coming morning and the resurrection of Christ," Marston says, no longer wearing the pale blue robes of Ex-Oh but the holy white vestments of a Caplain. He stands upon the driftwood dais, before the head of the deceased Caplain Amita. "Our beloved Caplain's resurrection will come at the end, for all of us, on the final day, when the Last Judgment is delivered, and when we take our last song to the depths. And, until then, we honor his name, he who first heard the word of God. He who gave us purpose. He who put our song into the deep."

Caplain Marston's voice, often cold and colorless, is filled with heat. Power in his speech that would rival Caplain Amita in the days when he had his full strength. Movement in his tall, hunched body.

"And today," he says, glancing at me—sea glass eyes burning like cold flames, "we honor his legacy with our song."

Antiphon: "*Quoniam omnes dii gentium daemonia at vero Dominus caelos fecit.*"

Chant: "*Ave Maria, gratia plena, dominus tecum.*"

Antiphon.

I lead, and though my voice does not break, it wavers under the weight of something. Something that threatens to close my throat. I fight back tears, looking at Caplain Amita's slender remains.

"Benedictus Dominus Deus Israel; quia visitavit et fecit redemptionem plebis suae."

Blessed be the Lord, God of Israel; he has come to his people and set them free.

To close, a hymn. A special hymn just added to the psalter, penned by Caplain Marston.

Like a dirge, it seems to my ears. Slow and heavy.

"By fire, may they be pur-i-fied

"By poison, may they see His light."

Finally, prayer.

"Laudate Dominum de caelis laudate eum in excelsis."

Praise ye Him, in the high places.

A prayer that comes from this, the lowest places.

Does that not make the praise even more special? More powerful?

If so, then I pray that Caplain Amita might know peace. That he, himself, be praised for being an instrument of God's will.

I am told I should take comfort in the face of death, and that I will see Caplain Amita again, in heaven, after the dead have been called from the ocean's depths. But, for today, he is simply dead.

The one person who knew the truth about me, who knew who I really was, has passed. And he has left me with a task that I am not sure I am capable of.

The key.

I feel its cold metal still burning my skin, tucked tight against my chest.

Caplain Amita said Marston would never suspect me, but I don't believe that to be true. His eyes narrow upon me at times. As though he's trying to see through me. Like he knows I have a secret.

And what will he do to me if he finds out? I'm not sure which secret I'm most frightened of him knowing.

After the hour is done, Caplain Amita's body is carried up to the Topside deck, where the elders and the anointed brothers will give him the final rights and, upon diving, commit his body to the sea.

I cannot be there for this rite. Me, nor the other Choristers. We cannot go Topside.

However, this marks the first time in days in which we are left to our own devices.

I slip away from Lazlo before he has a chance to notice I am gone, crawl down into the battery well, one of the very lowest compartments of the ship, where the air is close—a mingled smell of something acrid and metallic. Of fish rot and urine and other recesses. Few other than Caleb and I could fit down here into some of these spaces, for the room is filled by a massive bank of the heavy, block-shaped cells. At one time, the boat held a bank of thirty of these cells, and more in store to replace damaged ones, but now only twenty remain, several of which are seeping acid and are soon to fail.

Brother Ernesto doesn't trust Caleb enough yet to clean these essential elements. I must be careful to touch only the wood plank barrier as I climb down, avoiding the terminals. They are live. The shock would kill a person in an instant if they landed wrong.

So, it is I tasked with cleaning the corroded terminals. I keep the contacts and wiring dry. Pump away the standing, oily, brackish water into the bilge. My feet burn if I stand too long in that acidic brine. It's already eating away at the piping below, the very pressure hull. I remember once when we had taken on water from a burst ballast tank valve. The well flooded up to my waist. I had to pump for countless hours to keep the seawater from reaching the batteries.

If the water ever reaches the terminals, the electrical system will short. The boat will go dark. The *Leviathan* could be lost. Lost before its purpose is fulfilled.

I remove my robe, glancing through the hatchway above, making sure I'm not seen. I pull off my tunic, remove the key from its place, tucked against my chest inside my bindings.

I slip it into a crevice between a support strut overhead and the deck. I dare not keep it on my person, nor in my bunk or locker. Not with Caplain Amita dead and Marston in charge. Our bunks and personal lockers have already been searched for contraband.

Worse, Caplain Marston's God is somehow more wrathful and expecting than the God Caplain Amita bade us serve. The new Ex-Oh Goines, with his steely expression and tumorous neck, has become his enforcer. Always was a man even more exacting and severe than Marston, when he was just the Watch. Ten lashes given to Brother Micah for speaking when he should not. Twelve lashes to Brother Gregory for wasting food during his galley duty.

It's his new mission to remind the brothers and Choristers of our sacred, solemn duty.

To toil and to pray.

We Choristers have always been spared some of the harsher penance, but that cannot be guaranteed any longer.

I cannot step a toe out of line.

If they lash me, then they will see my bindings.

I must keep my bleeding hidden, when it returns. Surely it will. My curse.

A dry lump grows in my throat, thinking about Caplain Amita.

What a lonely feeling it is.

A hollowness in my tummy. Like a gutted rockfish.

I could tell Lazlo—I have thought of it before. I trust him more than anyone. He would keep my secret.

There might be a time when it's necessary for someone else to know. When I'll need help.

But not now.

Not yet, anyway.

I retighten the strip of linen about my chest, pulling the wrappings tight as I can. So tight I have trouble breathing. Round and round. That's how tight it needs to be in order to conceal my shape.

If I am to last long enough to fulfill the task Caplain Amita set upon me, the task God has chosen me for, then I cannot be found out.

———————

Today is a fishing day, a task that requires most brothers to be on hand.

"Must mean we're in a good, clean stretch of water," Brother Aegis says, pulling off his robes and tunic. The long scar that runs from his jaw to his temple gives him sort of a maniacal countenance when he smiles. A pink ripple. "No Topsiders."

It is no simple operation, fishing beneath the waves.

Brothers Aegis and Callum climb into the access port of the empty number eight missile tube, massive length of net folded and stored beneath them. And then the tube is flooded and the missile tube hatch opened on the top deck. Then they swim out, spreading the net. After, they must swim to the forward trunk, a task that requires holding their breath for up to five minutes.

The *Leviathan* drags the net along at low speed through shallow waters for a time, and then the nets are drawn back into the missile tube by winch, guided along by two other brothers. Sometimes Jacob, sometimes Martino.

All of it, dangerous business.

You can easily get snared in the nets, become trapped in the tube, or not make it back to the trunk before breath runs out.

Three have drowned since I've been aboard.

None for some time, though.

When the haul has been reeled in by winch and the missile hatch sealed, then the tube is pressurized again, the catch unloaded onto the deck of the chapel.

It normally takes no less than ten of us to pull out the haul; however, today, like the last several months, our catch is meager.

Skinny skipjack, smelt, a small reef shark, one baby bluefin, a handful of mackerel.

Brother Aegis, dripping, shivering, lips blue, crosses his arms around his skinny waist, frowning at the fruits of his labor. Sucks air through his few teeth. A whistle.

Ex-Oh Goines, who has been overseeing the operation, shakes his dour head. "The poison has finally reached our last fishing grounds. The day is drawing near, I fear."

No one dare respond to him, lest they wish to feel the bite of his leather lash.

He lumbers off, not helping us to collect the catch, or to roll and repack the nets.

"These aren't poisoned, nah," Brother Silas mutters under his breath as soon as we have carried the haul to the balneary, what was once known as the torpedo room, for cleaning, and it is just the three of us. Rare for him to speak outside of the mess, and especially a word of derision.

Lazlo shares a knowing look with me, eyeing the large, round-faced Brother Silas with great interest. A man whose eyes always seemed to be smiling, even on a day like today.

"How do you mean?" I whisper, untangling the flopping, rough-skinned skipjack.

The broad-shouldered brother takes the wriggling fish from my hand and holds its head to show me its eyes. Unmoving but alive, clear.

"See, not milky," he says, then he turns the fish and opens its gills so that Lazlo and I might see. The layered rows of the shark-teeth organ pulse and flex. "Its color is good, see? In't sick."

"Then why have the fish been so scarce?" Lazlo asks.

"Because," Brother Silas says, pausing for a long moment. So long a moment, I wonder if he will continue speaking at all. When he does, he leans in, serious: "Topsiders are pushing us out of the best fishing grounds."

"Seems like there are more of them than there used to be," I say.

Again, a moment of quiet reflection. Words unsaid. Something eats at him.

This is confirmed later, after supper. When the rumors begin to spread among the tables in the mess. Tonight, there will be a raid.

Of course, any real information must be paid for.

We trade and buy in teeth.

Things that have been lost but are still our own. Pieces of us.

Not all teeth are of equal value. Molars are worth more than incisors, but the quality of the tooth matters as well. Blackened ones are worth less than browned. Browned worth less than yellowed. Rare white ones—normally baby teeth—are worth the most.

I have managed to have kept most of mine which have fallen out—seven white baby teeth and five that have loosened since—and five others from trade. Takes more teeth to make a deal these days. That's because, since the worst of the scurvy has set in, there are more teeth to be traded. But also, it takes more teeth to make a trade, because goods worth trading for have become scarce.

Lazlo and Ephraim and I each sacrifice one of the best of our individual collection—two ochre incisors and a molar marred by only one blackened pip—and pass them along to Brother Leighton—one of the youngest brothers. Upon examining his payment and finding it suitable, he leans in and speaks conspiratorially.

"Brother Augustine an' me been asked to sharpen the blades, right? Readyin' flame jars and the like."

Brother Silas, seated at the adjoining table, listening in all the while, confirms the rumor with his silence.

"Praise God," St. John says, who had been sullenly scooping at the remainder of his watery broth with the back of his spoon. "We have not had any fruits or meat in . . ."

He cannot properly remember.

Neither can I.

"Will it be an island?" I ask. "Coconuts, perhaps."

"Mangosteen."

"Bananas."

A litany of words that conjure sharp memories.

I remember a time when, from the gleaming hatch of the conning tower—the halo of light—they brought down from their gathering a bushel of limes. They were still warm from the sun. They tasted like the light. Sweet and sour. My mouth wanted to collapse on itself.

Remembering those limes, my tongue tingles.

Normally, this would be a topic of some excitement, particularly for us Choristers, who never get to step foot Topside, but Brother Silas, brow already shelved and heavy, appears positively downtrodden.

"What troubles you, Silas?" Ephraim asks.

"No—no island," he says.

The jubilant mood is doused.

So, a ship raid, then. A raid on Topsiders.

No getting around it.

We have enough fish to last us a week, if we stretch, but we are low on all the other goods. Medical supplies, pantry items for the kitchen, fresh cloth and soap—whale blubber and ash is harsh, burns the skin—twine to repair the nets, oil for the engines, and other rarer but essential parts like gaskets and seals, and, if at all possible to locate, batteries. All of which have become more dangerous to acquire, since they can only be collected from Topsider ships, which are fiercely protected.

"We should launch the Last Judgment now," St. John says in his usual dictatorial tone, as though he, himself, might be the caplain. "End their miserable lives."

"They are wretched and should have our sympathy," Lazlo says.

"That's what old Caplain Amita thought," St. John says. "No, the Topsiders are sinners. Marauders. Caplain Marston has reminded us of that, yeah?"

"We were once Topsiders," I interject.

"And we were blessed. Purified. Thus, we should be careful to remain loyal and faithful, for our place in heaven is not fixed," St. John says, definitive, leaving no room for response. I look up and see him staring at me, an impish delight in his eye. A look that says, *Not even for you, Remy.*

I had only just come on board when St. John received his cutting.

The newly devoted are given two weeks to recover—the minimal amount of bedrest necessary, it was deemed, in order to have the best chance of surviving the procedure.

But that often wasn't enough time.

Many died from blood loss.

Some from ague. Infection.

St. John was stoic, even then. Would not let on the amount of pain he was in.

I found him one day, stumbled upon him in the storage compartment. Found him doubled over, heaving great, shuddering tears, blood pooling between his feet.

I had to help him then to his bunk, for he could not walk, and called for Brother Dumas.

He was muttering nonsense, I remember. His skin, burning hot. Brother Dumas feared that the ague would take him, as it had taken so many of the newly devoted.

I had seen these deaths. Heard them. Loud, mad passings,

as I lay in my bunk, when I turned eight years old, faking my own recovery.

So, I attended St. John, held his hand, when time and opportunity permitted, remaining by his bedside.

And he did not die.

The ague passed, and the bleeding stopped, at least for a time.

But the boy that was left was a cruel one. Particularly with me ... perhaps because I saw him weakened, as no one else had.

And he hated me all the more for it.

Nothing to do about that, I figured long ago. And the sting of his rebuke has long since faded.

I almost don't see Ex-Oh Goines step down into the mess—dour with the slight constant wink in his left eye, and the thick collar of tumular swelling about his neck. "Brother Lazlo," he says sharply. "A word."

Lazlo blinks. He looks at me as he slowly stands.

———————

"He's part of the raiding party?" I ask Ephraim, unbelieving. "Lazlo?"

The older Chorister is shocked as well. "That's what I just heard Brother Augustine say when they were making preparations."

I was curious as to why Lazlo had not returned to attend his afternoon duties.

"Why him, do you think?" I ask.

No Chorister this young has ever been sent Topside.

"Surely, there must be some mistake."

"Something to do with his knowledge of the electrics. Circuits and the like," Ephraim whispers. "Remember, Brother Calvert trained him up on fixing such things."

"Why not send Brother Ernesto?" I ask.

Ephraim only shrugs, disheartened as myself. "Come, we have to prepare."

To raid a Topsider ship, the *Leviathan* dives and then comes up from beneath the enemy on blown tanks, cutting engines so that it rises silently from the depths.

Leighton, Callum, Augustine, Silas—the strongest and youngest of the brothers—and now Lazlo, and Ex-Oh Goines himself, all comprise the raiding party. They have changed from their robes into trousers and tunics and hoods, all dyed a squid-ink black. Once the bulbs affixed to the bulkhead above the main hatchways begin flashing, they make their way forward, ready to exit up through the forward trunk hatch, at the top of the balneary, as soon as we've surfaced. They're armed with the few remaining firearms the boat can claim but mostly with knives—rust-spotted machetes and lengths of chain and jars filled with used oil with rags stuck into them. Grapples and hooks and coils of rope. Lazlo is given no weapon at all. His garb hangs about his lean body like loose skin.

I fight the urge to step forward, to speak to him as he passes. To send God with him. But now is a time for silence. Each in the line receive the cross in oil upon their foreheads, are given communion. Lazlo's face is wan, flat as he receives Caplain Marston's anointment.

Silas's face is tight and troubled as I've ever seen, and he has been on several boarding parties in the past.

It puts a sourness in my tummy.

When at last we are surfaced and the trunk hatch opened, I

watch as they disappear in a line up the ladder.

When the hatch is closed, we each attend our stations, ready to dive, ready to respond, waiting in the dimness. In the control room, Caplain Marston keeps an eye on the surface through the periscope, while Brother Marcus monitors the radar, and Brother Philip scans the sonar, with its radial arm raking the round, green screen, ready to ping any new enemy contact.

Myself, I straddle the hatch to the chapel, ready to check the bilge pumps in both compartments should we take on water.

We wait in what should be silent prayer, in meditation. But my mind swims in other, deeper, darker pools.

Lazlo. He is not short, not weak, but younger by far, and nowhere near so strong and able as the rest of the brothers in the party.

I once asked Brother Silas what it was like up there, on the surface.

Many of us had already posed this question—to him, because we knew him to be the most likely of any of the older brothers to answer—but he only answered when it was just he and myself, on kitchen duty.

"Topsiders, though—the marked—they deceptive, like. Trick you into feeling guilt for them. But you cannot have guilt for them if you wish to survive—they vicious. More vicious now than when I come aboard. I was your age, about. The war had happened, yeah. I lived on an island. A small set of islands called the Maldives.

"The poison. You hear about the poison, from the great war, you know. How it kills. Slow, like. But wan't poison got my people. Our island kept being raided by pirates—strangers from somewhere else. Evil Topsiders you hear about now. Accents I couldn't understand. Nothing we could do to stop them after a time. Did not know God then, as I do now. That's why I spared, yeah. They keep coming back, pirates. Finally, they took me one night. My family. Won't tell you what all they do to them, what they going to do to me, yeah. But then their boat was raided by the caplain, an' he showed no mercy. Took me aboard, though. Showed me God, yeah. Truth."

"What about the sun?" I asked him.

He squinted. "Don't remember much of that—only the elders can see the sun. But the moon, yes. Seen that. Plenty of that, on raids. Bright and round and blue-white. And the air. Rushes past your skin. Gives you chills," he said, hacking off the head of a skipjack in one heavy swing of a cleaver.

"What was your name?" I asked him. "Before you took the vow of the order?"

After all he had just confessed, this request gave him pause.

"I gave that name up."

"It's just . . . I don't remember mine," I said.

"Good," he said, swiping a large knife across the skin of the skipjack, scales flying every which way.

"I only remember an image. An image on a banner, I guess."

And I told him of the emblem that for some reason has remained rooted in my mind. Of the palm tree and the sea and the blue sky.

"Silas is a better name than my real one," he says. "Silas was a prophet. And you . . . you are named after a saint."

"Yes, St. Remy."

"Short for Remigius," he said.

"An ugly name," I told him. "In Latin, means *oarsman*."

"Ah, perhaps someday you shall row us to some safe shore, yes?"

"But what safe shore is available to us?" I asked him.

His smile faded.

Lazlo remembers his name. He was older than me, even though he was rescued from Topside shortly after I was.

Alden.

Alden Tomas.

He had two names. And he came from somewhere green, he remembered. And he had a mother who sang to him when it rained.

I think I must have come from an island too.

Though I remember so little.

Nothing but an image of a tree, and a sea, and a yellow-orange beach.

———

A wrenching sound brings me to. Metal on metal screech. A shudder. We've struck something. At the very least, we've side-swiped another vessel.

The klaxon blares shrilly, but we're given no order to abandon our current posts.

Another shudder, shouting from the deck above.

And then commotion forward, from the balneary. The raiding party has returned.

I abandon my post momentarily—just long enough to peek in through the hatchway.

The trunk hatch is opened, dripping water, and a prisoner, hands bound behind his back, a sack over his head, struggles, grunts as he is being dropped down through the narrow opening. Brothers Callum and Leighton struggle to contain his flailing legs. Once inside, the figure is led roughly aft by the two of them. I jump out of the way to let them pass. He is wearing a white uniform, this interloper from Topside, the short sleeve of his arm decorated with a colorful array of patches and symbols.

He wails, shrieks as he struggles against the men holding him. But no words. His mouth must be bound shut beneath the hood.

Never in my memory have we brought an adult prisoner on board. A Topsider.

Behind him, Brothers Ernesto and Augustine step down, and then I see Lazlo's short form among them. Alive. All of them are sweating—Ernesto's face bloodied. They fling several duffels full of goods to the deck. Supplies from the Topside ship. Coils of new, unfrayed rope. Jugs of water. A square package labeled INFLATABLE RAFT. Now they struggle to leverage in a heavier, more awkward package. Long, rigid.

When they release it, the sack crashes to the deck with a heavy thump, like it is filled with meat.

I look to the hatch opening, expecting Brother Silas to climb down at any moment, but Augustine is already closing up behind him, turning the hatch wheel.

"Sealed. Ready for dive!" Brother Callum cries out into the squawk box mounted on the bulkhead.

"What about Silas?" I say to Lazlo, whose chest is heaving from effort. "We can't leave without him."

And, yet, the dive bells are already ringing. I feel the hum of the *Leviathan*'s turbine in my toes. And Lazlo will not meet my gaze.

"Everyone to their stations," Brother Augustine says, wiping the sweat and blood and water spray from his forehead, rushing past me.

Lazlo follows, but I hook on to his arm, staying him, making him look at me.

Eyes wide, he glances toward the largest sack resting on the deck.

3

THE DEAD NORMALLY COME to the balneary, the forward-most compartment, for burial, carried on gurneys. If the body arrives already sewn up in a hammock, then they have come from aft, from engineering.

The Forgotten.

Young, limp bodies.

You can feel their bones through the canvas. Better when we cannot guess, when they could be anyone, or no one. We wear gloves when we handle these remains, for the poison which killed them—the reactor—can also poison you if you're in contact with it too long. That's what Brother Silas used to say. He would sometimes come to help us if the body was especially big and needed to be folded in order to be expelled through the torpedo tube.

Now it's Silas we must relinquish to the deep.

His round face somehow still wearing the faintest smile, even in the rictus of death.

Unlike the Forgotten, he is given a proper benediction. The elders, a few of the Brothers that knew him better, and the Choristers have crammed themselves inside the balneary, circling his big, stout body as much as the space will permit.

We Choristers—we slightly more holy, slightly more damned, are made to bathe the dried blood from Silas's wounds—three perfectly round holes clustered left of his sternum. Bullet holes.

Upon Silas's anointed body, Caplain Marston reads the rites as we draw the stitch through his nose. A sailor's custom of old. Make sure you're dead.

"Requiem aeternam dona eis, Domine."

After, when the elders and the caplain have taken their leave, we must dispose of the remains. They must be folded in order to fit inside the tube.

"Go on, Caleb," I say. He is already standing at a distance, just before the hatchway. He is too weak to be much use, anyway.

St. John is also of little help when it comes to folding, though he is the second oldest. In the end, he always turns away, and so it is Ephraim, Lazlo, and myself, accompanied by brothers Callum and Augustine, left to complete the task. They help us to turn Silas on his side, and lay the planks atop him, and then wrap chains about the planks and the torso, and then work the pulleys, closing the cinch tight until the clavicle cracks.

Next are the hips.

This is not him, I tell myself.

But, if our souls aren't freed from the sea until the day of resurrection, then isn't it? Are we not all trapped in our flesh until that day?

"Who killed him?" Ephraim asks Brother Callum when the deed is done and Silas's earthly remains ejected with pneumatic hiss and swish into the dark.

A question I have already asked Lazlo numerous times today. A question he would not answer.

In fact, he would not divulge anything about the raid at all.

He is discreet when it comes to Ephraim and St. John and Caleb, but never with me.

"Topsiders," the older brother who wears a patch across his left eye says, with the hint of the same accent you sometimes hear in Ephraim's voice. "Wretched bastards," he mutters, wiping his good eye. "Got 'em. Praise be," he says. "Got 'em, yeah."

"They got us, though," Brother Augustine says, round, red-faced, and portly, but perhaps the strongest of anyone on the *Leviathan*, especially now that Silas is gone. He wipes sweat and what must be dried blood from his roughly shaved pate with a grease rag that he then tosses to the deck. "And to make it worse, their helmsman steered right into the ship, tried to ram us."

"That's what that sound was," Ephraim says.

"We didn't take on water," I say.

"No, but the dive plane is jarred good. Got to help fix that now," Brother Augustine says, eyes red with salt. Exhaustion.

"Who is the interloper?" St. John asks, rather boldly, especially for him, who rarely suggests the slightest hint of impertinence, particularly in front of the older brothers. Augustine stops and shares a look with Callum, with Lazlo, who has remained silent all the while. The question all of us have been wondering. All of us gathered, curious as to why a grown man has been brought on board. A Topsider.

This, Brother Augustine is reluctant to answer. I offer a molar and two incisors from my stash, but he only waves his hand, not one to be easily tempted. "Someone Caplain says we needed. Said they was essential."

"Someone good with the electrics," Callum answers, clearly still upset, not worried a bit about what should or should not be divulged to us Choristers. "We hadn't had a good one of them since we lost Brother Calvert. Brother Ernesto in't up the task."

"And why were you sent, Lazlo?" St. John asks, apparently feeling bold enough to demand information.

Lazlo glances at Brother Augustine before answering. "Parts. Electrics. Wiring. I knew what we needed, helping Brother Ernesto like I do."

"A shame you could not do more to save Brother Silas," St. John says, smugly. Jealous, perhaps, that again, Lazlo was considered important enough to be singled out, to join on such an auspicious mission.

Lazlo looks down.

"We got what we needed," I say, trying to comfort him.

"Nah, wan't worth it," Brother Callum says bitterly, shaking his head.

Brother Augustine glances uncomfortably at us.

The ringing of the hull sweeps away the tense moment.

Call to Prime.

We will gather in the chapel, but today, since it is not a holy day, only for private prayer. Individual meditation.

Normally, Lazlo would linger at the back of the procession with me—sometimes to exchange a hushed word or two. I haven't yet had a chance to speak with him privately at all since his return. But he has rushed ahead.

We are almost to the chapel, and I have almost caught him, when the red bulb, caged in rusted wire, mounted above the main hatchway begins flashing.

"*Enemy ship!*" an urgent, crackling voice calls out over the squawk box. "*Dive! Dive! Dive! All unessential crew forward, to the balneary.*"

This is Ex-Oh Goines's voice on the speaker. Urgent, strained.

Though a rigid man, he has never been good at shielding his real emotions.

He is scared.

"We haven't fixed the dive plane yet," Ephraim whispers.

"Diving in't the problem," Brother Augustine shouts as he rushes against us to reach the ladder to the control room. "It's the surfacing I'm worried about."

"Topsiders," young Caleb says, rushing from the chapel, voice tremulous. "Again."

The deck pitches suddenly downward, and we all must grasp anything available to keep our balance—pipes, walls, the ceiling to brace ourselves as we carefully shuffle our way down the steeply pitched corridor.

No time to drop down into the battery well to retrieve the key. It should be safe, tucked where it is, even if there is flooding.

We snuff out lamps and grease wicks along our way, casting our path into a deep gloom. Gather buckets for bailing, should we need them. Finally, we make our way back into the balneary, completely dark, save for one bulb flickering above head.

More than just us Choristers here. Brothers Gonzaga, Marcus, and Erris. Alexander and Magnus and Philip and Nicolas follow. Some twenty of our sixty-eight-soul crew rush in.

More weight in the nose of the boat means we dive faster.

Lazlo huddles against me and Caleb.

If we are called to some other emergency service, like extinguishing a fire, or patching a breach, then we will have to move, but for now, we cluster together, a large mass, seated silently between the tubes, below the array of valves and dials and gauges.

One large, round gauge we are all keeping a close eye on. Depth.

A red needle arcs across the face, edging downward, past thirty fathoms now and still steadily falling.

Hollow knocks against the hull.

Pressure.

"I hope we don't stay down as long as that one time—I didn't like the way the air smelled. Made me dizzy as anything," Caleb says.

That time occurred when we were diving for Vespers, and the planes did not respond at all, stuck in a position that took us down and down. The *Leviathan* screamed at us that day. Groaned and creaked like I never heard. I was sure then that it would be our end, that we would be crushed. That's what Lazlo says will happen on our final day, after we launch the Last Judgment. The pressure will squeeze us tight until all the bolts and welds give. We went down to 140 fathoms before the Watch was able to regain control of the dive.

If the dive plane has been damaged, who is to say we can correct this time?

In the dark, the dank, green reek of the room closes in.

I hold my breath and listen. Listen for the splashes, for the inorganic thrumming of the enemy machines.

"Don't hear any depth charges," Ephraim says.

"No," I say, glancing at Lazlo. Something heavy in his gaze. "Not yet."

No sooner do I say it than a resonant *boom* thunders above us. I feel the percussion of the blast pass through the hull. Our little world rattles.

The deck lurches from beneath me.

But no sounds of cascading water from breach or leak. No

smoke, no fire. No damage-control alarm.

"It was shallow," Brother Marcus says, looking up with his normal, froglike frown. Like the rest of us, waiting.

"We should pray," Brother Ernesto, one of the feebler elders, says in his rich, quavering voice.

Yes, it is Prime.

A time for personal confidences with the Lord.

In the days of Caplain Amita, we were told to pray for those faithful who have suffered in the years of tribulation. People like my parents, who I do not remember in the least but who I figured must somehow still be deserving of Grace. To pray for the Demis and the rest of the Forgotten.

Caplain Marston now tells us to pray for our own souls instead. Those others are already damned, yet ours might still be saved.

Instead, I think of the bodies. Of Silas. Of Caplain Amita. Of Brother Calvert and all the others lost to sickness and raids and stale air and poison.

The truth is that I don't want to drown in the icy black fathoms.

I never have. Not even upon the promise of the salvation that will follow. A secret I have always kept to myself. If Caplain Amita really knew how I felt, he would have never entrusted me with the key.

Thus, just as during our times of private meditation, I often pray that we live.

I pray that all these seeping seals and pipes and valves hold true. I know that they are aging—these works, salt-corroded and rusted and gummed up and ailing. I do not want to suffocate—we have choked on fumes before. My lungs know the tight burn. So, I pray that the oxygen generator keeps sputtering away, the little brown strips taped to the vents still flutter, that the ventilation-fan system circulates the air. The CO_2 scrubbers once worked—machines and chemicals used to purify the air—now we use soda lime when we must, but even those stores have run out. We must surface often to vent. So, I pray that the diving planes and the rudder stay true.

I pray that we do not starve, for I know the pain of hunger. How it eats at the soul.

I pray our engine—our glowing blue heart that has sent so many Demis to early graves—continues to burn. For it powers everything. And should it fail, then we really would be doomed.

"We're going deep this time," Ephraim says, alarmed, despite his best effort.

Ninety fathoms.

A chain of muffled, watery, fizzling blasts rings weakly in the depths above.

"This is the third time in a month," St. John says, disgusted. Less fear in his voice than the others, perhaps. It's only for show.

The hull continues to groan around us. Echoes. Steady, deep drumming.

"It's a sign that our time has almost come, is what Caplain says," Caleb says soberly.

"Caplain Amita said that too," Lazlo says. "And we have survived this long."

Except we all know the truth.

That even if we survive today, it will only be to die some other day. We'll eventually take our last dive. Sing our last song, and let the depths take us.

But what about before then? What if we are damaged, or stranded under water before we have launched?

We were never officially trained in how to survive should such an event occur.

"Ditch," is what Brother Calvert told me one day, months before he went on a Topside raid and never came back. He said this to Lazlo and me, had gathered us together ostensibly to train us on properly cleaning and drying electrical parts, but he instead led us to the forward trunk.

"You can equalize the pressure in this air lock," he said, showing us the valves, how they worked. "This is how raids are sometimes done when we swim up while submerged. You can float right out if you ever get stranded below the surface."

He spoke hushed to us, knowing this was something we should not be taught.

"But what if we're too deep?" I asked him.

"Even at a depth of one hundred fathoms, a float or life vest will carry you right up to the surface—"

"What about air?" Lazlo asked.

"You'll have plenty in your lungs," Brother Calvert said calmly, answering our questions, seeming to understand our apprehension, our confusion. "Too much. You'll have to blow out as you rise."

"But should we survive?" I asked him, and everyone looked at me. "Should we try to survive?"

He didn't answer for a moment, considering his words, lowering his kind, warm eyes, rubbing together his big hands. He did that when he was contemplating. "Yes, I think you should always try to survive. It's in our nature."

"And what about after we launch the Final Judgment? The last days?"

Again, a long reach of silence.

Eventually, he said, "When that times comes, we won't need to worry about being saved, will we? We'll be lifted up into his Glory."

I see it now, the careful way in which he responded.

Is that what Caplain Amita believed as well? In the end?

That we should try to survive?

Lights spring on overhead, the red, flashing bulb cut off. The boat, still groaning unhappily, levels out.

One hundred and thirty-two fathoms.

It is as though all of us release a held breath at once. The very compartment sighs.

"*Return to your stations,*" the voice calls out over the squawk, distorted. "*Remain in readiness. Observe silence.*"

And that is all.

The red bulb flashes.

"We're not rising," Lazlo whispers, the last of us to stand, adding a glumness to the otherwise leavened mood.

"It's that interloper we brought aboard. It's his fault. He's a Jonah," St. John whispers in response. "Going to curse us all before we can complete our mission."

"We'll surface and vent soon," Ephraim assures, but appears to provide little ease for the dispersing crew.

Lazlo grabs my hand, staying me, pulling me back, eyes burning, frightened or curious, I am not certain. He swings the hatch shut after the last of the line of brothers has exited.

"What?" I ask, heart sinking just looking at him. "What is it?"

He wants to speak, to say something, but he won't. I see fear in his eyes.

"What happened up there?"

"They're not our enemy!" he says, speaking low—almost inaudibly. I think, at first, I must have misheard him.

"Who?"

He points up. "*The Topsiders.* They don't want to kill us."

"But . . . they've tried. They've dropped charges . . . They killed Silas. You were there . . ."

"I was there. I think this is only . . . retaliation. Because of what we did to the crew of the first ship."

"What did you do?" I ask, seeing the shadow fall across his face.

"We . . . we slaughtered them," he says, voice thin, high. He looks away. Shameful.

"They were Topsiders. The wicked . . ."

"But it wasn't a warship," he says, whispering, pulling me away from the door. "They called it a . . . research vessel. A ship called the *Janus.*"

"But they shot Silas . . ."

"They were defending themselves. We climbed up over the side—we struck fast—most weren't armed. We didn't kill them all at first . . ." He is shaking now as he grips both of my arms, the story spilling from him as though in one long breath. "Ex-Oh Goines gathered them all up on the deck, on their knees, tied cloth over their eyes. Asked each of them who was . . . who could work with the electrics, like. I had already done what was asked of me—I was shown these . . . circuit boards, here on the ship. Caplain Marston laid out different types for me to look for before we set out—told me where I should find them. In certain kinds of machines on board. So, that's what I do, once everyone is rounded up. Pick up some other equipment I was supposed to take if I could find. Time I come back on deck, most of the crew of the *Janus* has been killed. Blade at the back of the neck. The deck was all . . . It was bloody. It was pooled up. Pouring off the sides. Only a few left alive when I showed up. Ex-Oh was killing them, one by one, looking for this . . . specific kind of technician. And then . . ." Lazlo draws me even closer—swallows. "I *heard* them. They were crying, begging for their lives. They were saying things like . . . like the war was over. That the world isn't all poisoned. That they had kids back home. They were pleading for their lives, see?"

Lazlo finally lets me go, turns away to wipe his eyes.

"They're deceivers," I say, placing my hand on his shoulder.

But he brushes me away.

"I don't think so. They said they knew about us . . ." he says, eyes red with anger now. "Said they had been trying to track us, been trying to get in contact with us. Trying to tell us that they weren't the enemy. That we don't have to starve. That there's plenty of uncontaminated food. Enough for everyone, but Goines had each of them cut down anyway."

I brace myself against the bulkhead.

I'm suddenly aware of a gulf between us. A divide. Me, standing at the precipice of safe territory, and he, my best friend, on the brink of something altogether unknown and dangerous.

"No," I say, speaking through an uncomfortable tightness clenching in my chest. "It was deception, Lazlo. If they were contacting us, it was only a trick to get us to surface. To board us, to stop us from fulfilling our mission."

"I was watching from the hatchway," he says, shaking his head, seeming not to have heard me at all. "I saw it all. When the interloper—the one we brought on board—finally confessed that she was a technician . . ."

"She?" Have I heard him right?

He nods.

There has never been a woman brought on board.

I swallow.

"They're trying to keep it secret," he says.

"I can understand why."

"Ex-Oh says there was no choice. Once this woman said she was a technician, they killed the other two crewmembers."

There is no consoling Lazlo now. "He referred to Caplain Amita by name, one of the prisoners. Before he was killed. Called him 'Captain' Amita. Said that peace was at hand ... that they wanted to talk. To meet."

"How did they know the caplain's name?" I ask.

"I don't know," he says. "I'm not supposed to tell anyone any of this. Ex-Oh warned me. But ... I couldn't. I couldn't not say something to someone."

Now it's my heart that sinks. Heavy with its own, myriad secrets.

"What if we've been *wrong*?" he asks, a dangerous whisper. He takes in a great, shuddering breath. "What if the war is over? What if it wasn't the end of times?"

A clash of metal startles the both of us.

It came from the other side of the sealed hatch, followed by a muffled clapping, like the sound of retreating footsteps.

Lazlo and I share a lightning-fast, dread-deep look before I spring to the hatch and fling it open.

Down the corridor, into the mess and beyond, the lower deck is still active with the crew attending their duties. But no one retreating. No one near enough to have heard us.

On the deck, a wrench that must have been left on a small outcropping beside the hatchway.

We'd just imagined the footsteps. That's all.

"Come on," I say. "They'll have noticed we're missing."

I take Lazlo's grease-blackened hand and roughly pull him along with me.

———

Later that night, me in my bunk, Lazlo in his, directly below me, I feel his fingers brush against mine, from the inch of space between the edge of our bunk and the bulkhead.

In this gesture, he is asking if I am mad at him. If I still trust him.

A question I answer by interlocking my fingers with his.

The whales are singing out there in the dark ocean, their song resounding against the hull.

We lie awake and listen to them, Lazlo and I. Sometimes, when we are in the chapel, singing, the beasts sing back.

Here, though, this deep, it is quiet enough to listen to their solemn strains fully. Every odd sonorous leap and ululation. Every rich bellow and delicate turn. One calling out to the other in these blind, cold depths, the dark chambers of the sea. When all they have in the darkness is one another. Each other's song.

What were they discussing, these beasts? These leviathans?

"*Hello, I'm a whale,*" Lazlo whispers in a forced, deep timbre beneath me.

"*Hello, I'm also a whale,*" I respond, as deeply as I can, trying to stifle a laugh.

"*Do you have any fishes?*" he asks.

"*No, but I do have this man in my belly who keeps trying to get out,*" I whisper.

I hear Lazlo's smile in his breathing. I smile, too. For a moment.

But I keep thinking, do they have a message for me? Like Caplain Amita said? Will they tell me what I am to do, when the end finally comes?

I realize I am gripping Lazlo's hand too tightly. He doesn't seem to mind. I suppose he is gripping mine just as tight.

Sometimes, I dream we are whales, Lazlo and I. Free, and unafraid of the dark, of the depths. Places that are natural for us to go, singing songs that are not yet written. Together. Him singing a secret song to me, and me singing to him. A song only the two of us in the whole world know. Like our names.

Alden Tomas, I mouth but do not actually speak.

Someday, perhaps, I will remember mine.

4

TERCE.

The canticles sung at this hour are done so in *organum*.

Just two voices. One Chorister takes the lower melody, and one takes the upper, at an interval of a fifth. Together, they sing, at times, in a harmonic unison—beginning and ending on the same note. But in the middle, the upper register might do what Caplain Amita called improvising.

It is the closest thing to creation I've known. To owning something.

You have to trust your partner. Anticipate where their melody will wander. As Cantor, I take the upper melody. It is usually Lazlo who takes the lower.

But Lazlo hasn't yet taken his place beside me in the chapel.

At the tolling of the hour, Lazlo still not having arrived, Caplain Marston nods curtly to St. John, who eagerly steps before the psalter.

"Nunc Sancte nobis Spiritus."
Come, Holy Ghost.

Normally, singing, I lose myself. In the song, in the careful dance of melodies, the balance of harmony. This hour, indeed, often passes the quickest. However, my focus is divided. At first, concern for what punishment Lazlo will receive for arriving late. But, as the hour passes and still he does not rush to join the rest of the Choristers, a deeper dread begins to weigh in my belly.

As the singer of the top melody, it is my burden to embellish, to ornament and turn; however, St. John is taking liberties with the lower melody, so I must balance the duet, sticking closely to the more droning, center notes of the mode.

"Flammescat igne caritas."

Let fraternal love burn with fire.

When did I last see Lazlo?

Lauds. Afterwards, he was sent to the main deck to help Brother Ernesto with repairs. Was he injured? Even if he were in trouble for something, he would still be made to sing the liturgy.

Unless . . .

"Accendat ardor proximos."

Let ardor burn for our neighbors.

I glance sidelong at St. John when the canticle is done, when we are waiting for the recitation of prayers, but I cannot tell whether his expression is more or less haughty than usual.

Terce.

A time to invoke the Holy Spirit in order to bolster you. To give you strength to overcome the challenges of the day.

After the hour, in silent recession, Ephraim and Caleb share my similar, concerned expression. All except St. John.

I see it now. The smug grin on his face.

What has he done?

I find Brother Ernesto aft, sprawled on the deck of the first engineering compartment, working on the machine that takes seawater and runs a current of electricity to it, separating it into gases called hydrogen and oxygen.

Oxygen is what we breathe.

Hydrogen is dangerous, though. Flammable, which is why you have to be careful, skillful when working on it.

Brother Ernesto is none of these things.

Brother Calvert used to maintain this machine, as well as the CO_2 scrubbers, the dehumidifiers. These machines that he tended, he called the most important. And they need constant fixing. The scrubbers stopped working at full capacity years ago. It's one of the reasons we can only stay submerged for no more than a week at a time before venting. A task Brother Calvert took on with a quiet intensity and carefully taught Lazlo. Lazlo, in turn, has been teaching Brother Ernesto.

But Lazlo is not here.

"Cantor Remy," Brother Ernesto says, wiping the sweat from his forehead with the sleeve of his robe.

"Lazlo was supposed to be working with you earlier, yes?"

He frowns.

"It's only . . . you saw he wasn't at Terce," I say.

I glance behind Brother Ernesto, to the hatch that leads to the tunnel, the access to the reactor room, to the engine room. This barrier no one save the elders or a handful of the brothers can cross. Where the Forgotten dwell. Not that anyone in the forward compartments would want to enter. There isn't even a guard posted.

Brother Ernesto follows my gaze. Squints heavily.

St. John. He must have been listening to everything Lazlo said yesterday. He must have told the caplain. Of course he told.

"Lazlo was a good boy," Brother Ernesto says, looking down, shaking his head. But this is all he will say. He seems ready to move on.

They are not to be spoken of, those who are sent back.

They are to be forgotten.

Lazlo.

Sent back to toil. To slowly poison himself in the reactor compartment.

I think of the thin, faceless frail bodies I have loaded into the torpedo tubes.

"But this is wrong ... Why ... He didn't do anything wrong ... He doesn't deserve this," I say. My knees go weak. No tendons. I cannot keep standing. It's as though all of the energy in me has suddenly evaporated.

I fall to the ground, can't seem to catch my breath.

It's as though there's the weight of a sailfish pressing upon my chest.

I feel Brother Ernesto's hand upon my back.

"Child," he whispers, intently, urgently, "it is a terrible thing, but you must not do this."

He grabs my chin, forces me to face him. Looking serious now, holding a blackened finger to his dry lips.

"You should get back to your duties," Brother Ernesto whispers. "Collect yourself. Don't let anyone see. Off you go. Use the lower deck ..."

But before I can move, a figure steps in through the hatchway.

Ex-Oh Goines enters, head half-ducked, giving Brother Ernesto an admonishing look, one thick eyebrow raised.

Then his heavy, dark eyes level upon me. A withering look that makes me feel the heat of shame. He stares at me silently until I stand. I wipe my eyes, but it is clear that he knows I have been crying. And, of course, he knows that I am not at my assigned station.

"Cantor," he whispers curtly. I can only imagine the words that will follow.

"Caplain will have a word with you," he says. "Brother Ernesto, you are needed in the chapel."

Ernesto refuses to look at me as he nods respectfully, wipes his hands.

Fear of being associated with me.

I'm next, I think.

First Lazlo, and now me.

———

A high, raspy voice bids me to enter.

Inside, the quarters are different than when it belonged to Caplain Amita. Far more spare. The shelves of books are gone, as are the illustrations of the saints, the charts of ocean and coast. Now a single crucifix adorns the wall, the lamps and grease wicks casting a long shadow of Jesus's broken body. Solemn and austere.

Caplain Marston sits at his desk as though it has always been his, back turned to me, scribbling something on a large sheaf of parchment while I wait in silence.

Crude notes arranged upon staves.

"Cantor," he finally says before even stopping with his notating. Eventually, he does turn, folding his long fingers together at his lap. On his face, a most uncharacteristic smile. Were it to be found on the face of any other man, I could mistake it for genuine. But here, on this face, something wrong in it. He says, "I invited you here because I know how ... close you were with Caplain Amita ... the relationship you shared. You must be feeling quite a weight still so soon after his passing."

"Yes, Caplain," I say softly, carefully. Not the response I had expected. My knees still feel weak beneath me. I try to slow my breathing.

"You shared a confidence with him," he says.

"I did. Indeed."

"I wonder, Cantor, if we might build a similar relationship. A similar trust . . ."

I see the key hanging about his neck on a chain. The false missile key. He continues. "For you see, Cantor, I think there might be something . . . weighing upon your soul. Something you might need to confess."

My heart races. Does he know? That I'm a girl? About the key? Did Caplain Amita tell him these secrets before death took him?

"Chorister Lazlo," the caplain says.

My face burns hot. The lump in my throat has grown. Big as a stone I can't swallow.

An expression of great, disingenuous pain crosses the caplain's face. "He is sick, I am afraid, Cantor. Sick, and there is only one place for him.

"I blame myself, partly," he continues. "You see, there's a reason why we don't send Choristers Topside. A reason why we normally send the . . . seasoned. The steadfast faithful. For the work that we must do is indeed bloody. Wrathful. And the Topsiders are deceitful at every turn. Their lies are like a disease. Their ideas. You see, some ideas can be an even worse sickness than one that ails the body. A sickness of the mind. Of the soul. Dear Lazlo confessed this to me. Confessed the . . . heretical thinking that might tear apart our order in these, our final, our most important days. You see, if one part of the body fails, so do the others. Like this very machine. The *Leviathan*.

Every function important to the whole."

Something darker in his eyes now, the way he is looking down his long nose at me. "Like the Demis and the other Forgotten, he must be purified by the presence of God. By the energy that drives us. His light."

Caplain Marston lifts his chin as he says these last words, eyes closed, as though in prayer. Then he stands, approaches me, places a lank hand on my shoulder. "Now I must ask you a question."

My heart races. Thrums.

He rounds behind me. "Cantor Remy, I know you were close with Chorister Lazlo. Please tell me . . . did he confide any of these . . . sick thoughts to you? I assure you, you will not be punished for speaking honestly with me."

I fight the urge to recoil. To break down right here and now.

He already knows—if St. John told him about Lazlo, then he has told Marston that I was the one Lazlo was speaking to. So, he will know if I lie. But if I tell the truth . . .

"He did confess some . . . dark thoughts to me, Caplain," I say. "I'm sorry I did not tell you immediately. I was just . . . I was worried for him."

Caplain Marston circles around to face me, peering down at me, head hunched. "And what exactly did he say?"

The truth. That's the only way out of this.

I clear my throat. "He said that . . . he wondered if we'd . . . if we'd been wrong, this whole time. What if the war was over? What if the Topsiders weren't evil after all?"

The caplain nods thoughtfully. "What an easier, kinder world this would be were that true. And what did you tell him?" he asks, turning away, slowly pacing the length of the cabin.

"That the Topsiders were deceivers, of course. That they

were trying to . . . evoke guilt from him. I told him . . ." *Breathe!* ". . . that he shouldn't be saying such things."

"And rightly so," Caplain Marston says, finally ceasing his slow pace, turning on his heels, standing squarely before me, crossing his arms. "Your will is strong, Cantor. This is why you have risen to be the prime voice of our chorus. Unlike Lazlo, I know you are no lost soul. Your faith, steadfast. Your voice is a divine gift—lifts the heart of every man here. Every soul, into the light."

There's that dark light in his eyes again, though I'm not sure if it is the fire of conviction. In fact, I'm not sure that he believes me at all. But that doesn't seem to matter.

"Perhaps Lazlo told you something about the interloper we've brought aboard as well?"

Did St. John hear all of what Lazlo confessed to me?

"He did . . . he did tell me something about the prisoner," I say.

"Indeed, the interloper we have brought on board is a female."

That very word—*female*—strikes a new, icy chord down the middle of me.

"You understand," he says, "we must keep silent. It would confuse your fellow Brothers and Choristers. We would not have brought this woman on board if not absolutely necessary. And she will be expelled as soon as possible. Tell me, have you shared this or any of the other ideas Lazlo confided in you?" he presses. "His doubt?"

"Of course not, Caplain. I wish I had not heard it myself," I say. The tears begin to well up, unbidden, once more.

"It is okay to mourn, Cantor Remy. I, too, was fond of young Lazlo . . ."

"Perhaps his punishment need not be so severe—I know Lazlo . . . I knew him well. He has never faltered before." The words fall out of my mouth before I can stop them. "Caplain," I add, the appropriate decorum.

Caplain Marston presses his lips together—perhaps taken aback at first—then closes his eyes, nods heavily, as though this is all a burden, a weight on him. "Always the fearless heart. You know as well as I there is no way for him to return. He must remain. We must all be spiritually resolved on the day of the Last Judgment.

"No," he says, seating himself once more, "you may pray for him, Cantor. Pray for his soul. It might be purified and saved yet."

"Th-thank you, Caplain," I say wiping my eyes. But gone is the sadness. I feel a heat building inside me. A quaking.

The caplain continues. "In his final days, you may have noticed that Caplain Amita was also not himself as well . . ."

"Caplain?"

"He, too, might have also confessed to you some . . . notion of a crisis of faith. Sometimes, you see, it's as easy to lose heart at the end of a life as it is in the middle. Especially when you don't get to see a vision through to its end."

"No . . . no, I don't believe so. Caplain Amita has never faltered in his faith . . . that I know. Not in my presence."

A sigh.

Perhaps disappointment.

Perhaps he knows I am lying. But, instead, a counterstep—"I mean not to tarnish the legacy of a great man. You will forgive my own candor . . . but it is as though I feel we two can speak honestly."

Another smile. That makes my gut twinge.

"Things will move fast now, Cantor," he says, turning back to his large sheaf of parchment. "The hour of the final judgment draws near. We must all prepare."

———————

When I return to the forward compartment, to the balneary, I find Ephraim and Caleb and St. John pounding old linen in the slurry vat for the making of parchment. They look up at me.

Caleb and Ephraim are both visibly relieved—they must have thought I'd suffered the same fate as Lazlo. Perhaps I almost did.

St. John's expression is unmistakably dour.

I take up a mashing paddle and join them, opposite St. John, who is glaring down into the vat.

"We were worried . . ." Caleb whispers, next to me.

"All is well," I say. My hands shake as I pound at the tub of turbid, greyish water.

"L-Lazlo," he whispers, even more softly. A question.

"We don't speak of them," St. John snaps, slinging a narrow look at me from across the vat.

Caleb goes pale.

Ephraim looks to St. John and then to me, cautious, as though expecting that I might take up my paddle and strike St. John down.

I want nothing more than to bring it across his smug face.

It takes everything in me not to. A red-hot steam.

But I know now that these are dangerous times. That I can't risk being found out. Not if, as Caplain Marston says, our time is nearing the end.

St. John almost seems disappointed.

I pound at the mash vat with my paddle. A slurry cloud billowing—larger bits of linen floating, swirling in the water. Bright white. Cleaner than any of the old linens we would normally use.

"Where did this new cloth for parchment come from?" I ask.

"The interloper," Ephraim says. "Caplain said they'll make fine, strong parchment."

"Also had these colorful adornments on them," Caleb says, frowning. "Wanted to keep one, but St. John said I couldn't."

"You don't want anything to do with Topside trash," St. John says.

"What sorts of adornments?" I ask.

Ephraim glances at St. John before handing over the crate filled with the refuse that will eventually be ejected through the torpedo tube at the day's end. Atop, an array of pieces cut away from the interloper's uniform.

Silver-colored buttons and bars. Stripes.

And then a few of the patches I'd caught sight of briefly the last evening, on the interloper's sleeve. A colorfully vibrant bit of round cloth.

My throat tightens.

A vivid blue sea. Yellow land, a palm tree with green leaves. The embroidered white letters at the base: *CPN.*

This image I have seen before. This image from my childhood.

"I heard from Brother Duncan that the interloper was brought to the chapel today," Ephraim says. "I think it's something to do with the Last Judgment."

"Is it broken, do you imagine?" Caleb asks.

"It is not broken," St. John says, knowingly. "It will fire true, guided by God's hand."

"Then why was a Topsider brought on board in the first place?" I ask.

"It's the caplain's business," St. John replies curtly, effectively ending the line of conversation.

St. John must not know the interloper is a woman. He must not have heard that part when he was listening in on us. I doubt he would be speaking of the matter at all if he knew.

"I wonder where he's from," I say. I didn't mean to say it. The thought just spilled out.

"Does it matter?" St. John asks sharply.

"I don't understand about Lazlo," Caleb says, heart still painfully fixed on the topic.

"He lost his faith," St. John answers before anyone else can. No mistaking that twist of delight in his tone. "And that can't be abided. Doubt must be burned out of us. Of course, I suppose some of us are cleverer at hiding our true feelings, aren't they? Our transgressions?"

That barb is directed at me. At least I know I've gotten under his skin.

I look down again at the patch, wanting to hang on to it, to this memory that has been made manifest. That I am holding in my hands.

But, no, they'll see. I toss it back into the bin. Take hold of my paddle once more.

———

After prayers, we sit down in the mess for what should be the grandest meal of the day. It has never been so meager.

Mushroom cake with a thin broth of fish. No bread, of

course. Nothing of substance that might fill the stomach.

I cannot bear to take more than a few spoonfuls.

Brother Dormer trades me a tooth for the rest of my meal. A molar. Yellowed, but not pocked with rot.

A good trade.

Based on the rules agreed upon by the Choristers, we should divide Lazlo's stash between us, but I suggest that we hold on to them, in case he comes back. Only St. John disagrees, but he is powerless in this decision.

Though the others will not say it, I know what they're thinking. Lazlo will not come back. They never do.

I will collect all the teeth I can, and might just have enough to pay for a potentially dangerous request.

Only a select group of brothers are allowed admittance past the tunnel. Brothers O'Shea, Theodore. Brother Dormer is one of those who ferries meals to the back, Dormer, who is kind if not dense. Dull in the eyes.

He is the one most likely to carry back a message to Lazlo, for the right price.

The only question is what my message will say. Brother Dormer cannot read, as is the case for most of the second generation of crew brought on just after Caplain Amita delivered God's wrath. I can write anything I want, and it will be private. Words of hope? What consolation could I bring?

We all know the fate that awaits the Forgotten.

"They sleep in hammocks, like," Brother Theodore once told us. "In a compartment behind the engine room. Lowest level. All damp. All crammed together. Worse than the way we're packed in here, yeah. An' they work the machines, like. They chained up. The smallest work the reactor. Got to have water pumped into the core almost all the time. They given these suits that supposed to keep them from getting poisoned. But they don't help after long. Yeah. They got to control the pump by hand. Control how hot the reactor burns. That's what gets them. Suit don't help when it burns hot."

They lose all the hair on their bodies. Their skin becomes riddled with sores. They swell. They cough up blood.

They eventually die, from the inside out.

"Have you seen him?" I ask Dormer when the mess has cleared. "Lazlo?"

His eyes dart away. He gets nervous sometimes. He sits and rocks when he gets nervous.

"I know we aren't supposed to talk about him." I offer him another two teeth. A molar and an incisor. Pristine. Barely yellowed.

"Yeah, seen him," he says, softly, running the pad of his index finger over his newly gotten tokens. He frowns.

"It true that he was sent back because he was planning on trying to escape?" he asks.

"No," I say. "Nothing so bad as that," but I don't tell him the rest. "As far as I know."

"Where do they have him?" I ask, swallowing.

He, too, is saddened by Lazlo's punishment. Everyone liked him.

But he doesn't answer.

His silence tells me.

Lazlo doesn't have much time.

———

In my bunk, I press my ear against the hull.

There's a whale calling, out there in the darkness, faintly. If there are two, I do not hear the other. Just one voice looking for another, seeking with blind eyes. Not able to find them.

Lazlo.

Poor Lazlo.

I won't let myself imagine what he might be experiencing right now.

Never before has a Chorister been punished so severely, unless their voice failed them.

Having utility, talent, the ability to praise Him with voice has always been enough to spare us before.

And then the logical question that will not quit my mind—that keeps knotting up my heart. Why would the caplain so vehemently try to keep Lazlo silent if there wasn't some truth in what he said?

There is one person who might know the truth.

5

THERE ARE FEW TIMES during the day when the boat is quiet, when you could cross from the balneary to the chapel without meeting a fellow brother. During prayers is one of those times. Of course, there would be no opportunity to slip away then. No, the only time is before the hammer is brought against the hull, between the hours of Compline and Matins.

During first sleep.

So, I lay awake in my bunk, waiting for the rhythmic sound of my fellow Choristers' slumbering breaths.

Then I climb down from my bunk, search with my toes for the deck without making noise.

There are plenty of sounds to mask my footfalls.

Indeed, the mess—the galley is loud as always, Brother Dumas readying the next day's broth. Hisses. The heavy *thwock* of the cleaver. Someone always mans the radio, just as with the sonar, the helm, the periscope, especially when the ship is surfaced for venting, when it is at its most vulnerable.

Here, I must slip past quickly.

Past the radio room lies Silas's old quarters, and then the wardroom, where the elders congregate for their own meals. It is almost always occupied by one or two at any given hour. Quick. Not a breath.

Once I reach the chapel, I light a grease wick, make my way beneath the lower deck, through the lowest part of the boat, where I am often sent, tasked to crawl through the narrow and wet, oily underworks in order to inspect the pressure pipes, hoses, cables, on the hunt for signs of rust or corrosion or seepage.

I step lightly, hunched over, trying not to slosh through the pools of stagnant water as I inch my way forward, careful not to douse my wick—the tiny flame casting just enough light to navigate. I know these underworks better than anyone. Where every conduit and hose and cable leads. The location of the access plates. I find the one I'm looking for above me, the cell in which all who are in need of correction, of discipline, are sent for days of meditation, for prayer and reflection.

These are meant to be times without food or water, without distraction, but I found a way around this some time ago, when Lazlo was locked inside for the whole of a week due to his tardiness in arriving in line for Lauds.

Another of Marston's punishments. Yes, God could be vengeful, and yes, I was contravening a direct command, bringing a few meager victuals to my friend. But a punishment like this . . . it just didn't seem right. Not when life was so difficult to begin with.

Here, in this narrow chamber just above, is where the prisoner is being kept.

This woman.

This interloper with the patch I have seen before. The image that, when closing my eyes, I remember as clearly and vividly as anything.

I unscrew the rusted plate, carefully, softly as the corroded metal will allow. Once it is removed, a mass of bound wiring spills out. Above that, a grating, the gaps of which are only big enough to pass the smallest morsel of food. I can just see up into the darkened chamber by the light of my flame. No sign of the prisoner. But I can smell the human inside.

"Where do you come from?" I whisper up into the darkness. I'm not sure if she is sleeping, if she has heard me. Then I hear a rustling. Sudden, cautious movement.

"Down here," I whisper. And then I hear the popping of joints, and, by my dim wicklight, wide, gleaming eyes appear on the other side of the grate above.

"Who ... who are you?" the interloper asks. Voice raspy. Parched.

Is this a woman? Yes, this voice sounds different than the others.

Cleaner. Higher.

Is this the way my voice will sound? If so, then I will eventually be found out.

"What does the image on your patch mean?" I demand. "What does *CPN* mean? Tell me, and I'll give you some water."

"Patch ..." she asks, confused, voice trembling, but louder than I would like.

I shush her. "The one with picture of the tree and the beach and the ocean."

"Hm," she grunts. "The emblem for the Coalition of Pacific Nations. CPN. Comes from the old flag of Guam. Have you seen it before?" A new, careful excitement in her voice.

"What is Guam?" I ask.

"An ... an island. It was the strategic base—" She stifles a cough. "One of the last strongholds for American forces after the first war. Now it's the northernmost seat of the Coalition. It's where I was stationed. Where I set sail from."

This stream of words means little. The places, these terms. But America. A word spoken of only in the past tense. A place that was. One side of the great war. Where the elders all came from. Caplain Amita told me all about it.

"I thought America was destroyed," I say.

Silence for a moment. "Large parts of it are . . . now. Please. Water."

I had almost forgotten. I feed one end of a rubber tube up, through a gap in the grate, and place the other end inside my canteen containing the half of my water ration I saved this evening.

I hear her slurp down two big gulps.

"Easy," I say. "You'll get sick."

I hear her fast breaths.

"My name is Adolphine," the interloper says, still heaving.

Her accent is different than anything I've ever heard. Thick. Long *e*'s.

Adolpheen.

"What is your name?" she asks.

I hesitate.

"You're just a child," she presses. Not a question. "You've seen this patch before?" she asks, shifting her tack once more, desperation in her voice.

"I remember it . . . from before I was saved," I finally say. I shouldn't be speaking with her, I know. I shouldn't be out of my bunk. If I am caught, then my fate will be undoubtedly the same as Lazlo's. But I can't help it. I have to know.

"Were you trying to kill us?" I ask.

Silence. Her gleaming, dark eyes appear above me again, just on the other side of the grate. I cannot make out the rest of her features. All obscured in darkness.

"No. No, we were not," she says. "We came to try and help you . . ." Her voice is tight with tears. I hear her sniffle. "We'd been hailing you for weeks, tracking you. We know that you are hungry—most of your food routes have been cut off . . ."

"And how do you know that? How do you know about us at all?"

"It was one of you who told us everything. Told us all about your boat. A man named . . . Calvert. That was his name."

I suck in a breath. "Brother Calvert. He died. Died during a raid Topside."

"No, he didn't. No, he escaped. Made it look like he died in order to flee. I remember meeting him. Looked like a ghost, he was so pale. Thin. Scurvy had already taken him. He lasted a few months in our infirmary back in Guam. But he told us . . . everything. Everything."

"Lies," I whisper. They must be. Why would Calvert just leave us like that? Betray us?

But Adolphine presses: "The *Leviathan*. That is the name of your boat. Calvert told us about your order. Your prayers. How they b-butcher the boys. It's called castration, what they do." She says it in a way that says, *I know this happened to you.* "They force some of you to work in the reactor room. He told me about the missile." Her face is pressed down against the grate. Her skin is the color of brown coconut husk, I can see by the flickering flame in my hand. A darker shade than Lazlo's skin. Than mine.

"The Last Judgment . . ." I say, and the words sound odd on my lips.

"It doesn't work, though . . . the missile," this woman named Adolphine says. "Calvert. He was the electrician for the ship, yes? He told us . . . the missile wouldn't fire. Some part of its targeting system has been faulty since the first days of the war. Told us that your Captain . . . this Amita . . . he knew it wouldn't fire. That's why we decided to try and reach out to him. We were trying to reason with him . . . trying to get him to come in. To bring all of you in, to safety."

I could not speak if I wanted to. This river of information, inundating. Spilling over me.

"That's why I've been taken," Adolphine says. "Your brothers . . . they lined us up on the deck of our ship and took turns executing us. They were asking who knew electronics. I . . . I kept myself from being killed. I volunteered. In order to stay alive." Her voice, so soft, cracks, pained with guilt. "But I won't fix it. I will die first."

She pauses.

Footsteps sound on the deck above. Brother O'Shea, patrolling the central corridor of the chapel. I can tell by the weight, the particular gait in every footfall. He pauses a moment, right outside the cell above, by the sound of it, and then continues on.

"You were probably taken from a Guam boat when you were young," Adolphine continues, quieter than before. "That's where you must have seen the symbol."

"I . . . I was saved. We were all rescued from the Topsiders. The wicked."

A dark sort of laugh. "This boat has been kidnapping boys for almost twenty years. Malaysia, Indonesia, Oceania. Australian ships. I grew up on Guam, hearing about the raids."

No. No more!

I replace the plate, begin screwing it back into place.

"*Wait!*" she hisses.

But I do not.

"*The world didn't end,*" she continues, her voice only slightly raised, muffled. Only just quiet enough to be quiet. But the words still audible. "People survived. More than half the world is still alive. Some lands are poisoned, but many are not. Much of the radioactive fallout has settled out of the atmosphere. There's been war, but now we're on the brink of peace. *We have survived. You have to tell people this . . . we are not your enemy!*"

I can listen to no more.

But that word haunts.

We.

———————

"What?" I ask Ephraim, who has been giving me furtive glances all morning.

"You got up last night, before Vespers," he says, softly, even though we are alone for the moment in the balneary. The one among us who observes silence most ardently. He's helping me to dump the steamed bits of fish—guts and gills and eyes—into the wide tub we use for oil pressing.

"Ex-Oh Goines asked me to check on one of the bilge pumps, below the chapel," I say, not looking at him, hoping he will not see the lie in my eyes.

He accepts this excuse without question, but I'm not convinced he believes it.

"You must be tired," he says as we hoist the hundred-pound weight by pulleys and lower it over the tub.

"Very," I say.

I did not sleep at all upon slipping back into my bunk. Could not.

Not after everything the interloper said to me.

Out of everything she told me, it was a question that burned in my mind, kept my eyes open to the dimness.

The missile. The Last Judgment.

Why would Caplain give me a key to a missile he knew would not work? Perhaps he intended for us to finish our mission.

The reverie is broken by the appearance of Brothers Jessup and Ignacio, each carrying an end of a long, canvas-bound package.

A body. That it is sewn up in a canvas hammock means it has come from aft. The form inside is small, light in their arms.

They deposit their delivery upon the table and exit without a word.

I feel, inside the frayed, brown and yellow and green stained sack, the body, the hard, thin limbs. The shape and size, familiar.

I freeze.

Ephraim and I share a look. He doesn't stop me as, heart pounding, cold building in my belly, I tear open a bit of the seam at the corner of the head of the pouch. Just enough to peer inside. I brace my heart for the reality that it will be Lazlo's lean, pale bronze face staring up at me—but . . . it is not.

This is Bartholomew.

A Demi who was cast back into engineering months ago. Bartholomew, who had survived his cutting, and had a lovely, deep and smooth voice until he did not. Until the voice cracked, soured. He is barely recognizable. Face gaunt, skin stretched across the skull. Eyes hollow and sunken. Cheeks and chin speckled with sores. Red lips. No hair except for in scrawny tufts.

The smell of death chokes me. I gag, must turn away. Ephraim as well. Only after we've regained our breath, taking a step away from the fetid stink, do we finish the job, covering him once more. We hoist his body carefully into the torpedo tube. It fits easily, he is so slight. Then we seal and pressurize, and, upon reciting our prayers respectively, I open the torpedo tube doors, and Ephraim hits the firing trigger.

Hiss.

Fizzle.

Another soul relinquished to the sea.

Ephraim places his hand squarely upon my shoulder. His commitment to silence is, in this instance, a comfort.

The moment is broken by the harsh ringing of the hull.

Sext.

The midday hour. The part of the day where the light should be shining on us fully, were we standing out in the open air.

God's light, bathing us.

We sing Kyrie eleison.

Lord, have mercy.

Caplain Marston speaks—our lesson for the day, one that is different than Caplain Amita's message that we were to pray for the Topsiders. For those who are suffering during these long years of tribulation.

No, Marston's message is harsh, even in the hour of the Kyrie. Mercy has already been delivered to those who have deserved it. So, in this time, we instead praise the penitent. Those who have done God's work. To acknowledge the mercy God has shown us, particularly we Choristers, who were saved. Who were purified.

Lord, have mercy.

But there is no mercy here on this ship.

Lazlo was penitent.

He was kind and good.

And he is being punished. For what?

All because he discovered the truth. That, maybe, not all the Topsiders are evil. That, perhaps, they were even trying to help us. That there is still a world up there, even after we unleashed God's fury.

And, if this prisoner Adolphine is telling the truth—*if*. She might not be. She might only be feeding me lies in order to try and save her own skin. Caplain Amita knew the missile wouldn't fire, and he never tried to find a way to fix it. He never planned on delivering the Last Judgment.

Does this mean that he lost faith in the end?

It's a question that makes my stomach turn.

Was I stolen? Taken away from parents who might have loved me? Were my parents killed, like so many others, at the hands of my fellow brothers? All by order of Caplain Amita himself. A man who I have revered above all.

I know only one thing for certain. He entrusted the key with me, not Marston. He entrusted me with it because he did not trust Marston. Caplain Amita told me as much. That Marston would not hear the call from God when the time eventually came.

The caplain didn't destroy the key, though. He could have done that. Could have thrown it into the sea, to ensure the missile would never be fired.

No, he truly meant, if the time came for the missile to be fired, it should be my choice. But why mine?

"Where are you from?" I ask, looking up once more through the grate, into the darkened cell above.

I shouldn't be here. It was risky enough, slipping away once.

It's one thing if Ephraim noticed—he would not go to Caplain Marston. But St. John certainly would.

Still, it is too important.

The prisoner stirs. Moves sluggishly.

"Ah, the little bird returns to my window," Adolphine says. Maybe an attempt at humor, but a weak one. Weak, strained like her voice. I slip through the gap in the grating a slender slice of fish cake.

When she realizes what it is, she takes it from my fingers quickly. I hear her chew, savor it.

Then I snake the water tube up.

"Thank you, child," she says after taking a long drink, relieved, some of her energy renewed.

"I've never heard someone talk like you. Sometimes, when new kids join us, they have all kinds of different ways of speaking. Different shades of skin. Do they speak that way on Guam?" I ask.

"I am not from Guam. I was born on an island in the Caribbean called Martinique. The Caribbean ..."

"I have seen charts for those islands," I say. "Caplain Amita showed them to me."

"After the war, my family was evacuated to Panama due to radiation from the Cuba strike. And then my parents joined the American armed services—we heard that there was food and opportunity for those who served. Both my father and my mother were soon engaged in the Pacific fleet, which was based in Guam, and they brought me along."

"You have brothers and sisters?"

"Three ..." she answers. "Three brothers."

"Are they alive?"

"One is. He's stationed at Base Darwin, in Australia. One

was killed in the battle of Oceania, just last year. The other died when I was very young. Typhus. Child," she says, after a pause. "Why are you asking me these questions?"

"They let women serve ... they let women serve with men on your boat?"

"They do. There was a time, before the war, when they did not. But now, every person must serve. In order to survive."

A woman.

I still cannot believe it.

I cannot remember ever speaking with a woman.

"My name is Remy," I tell her. "It isn't the name I was born with. All those brought aboard, we were given different names. Sacred names."

It feels like a confession of my sins, divulging all of this. As though she is playing the role of confessor. The role Caplain Amita often played for me.

Adolphine doesn't respond for a time; I hear her shift. I think she is lying down, curled, for there is no room to lie flat in those tight quarters. She presses her face against the grate, like last time. I see one eye in this dimness, looking down at me through the mass of exposed wiring, big, honey-colored, and red-veined.

"Remy, I think you will get in trouble if you are found speaking with me," she says, sober, tired.

"I need for you to tell me about the war," I say. "And what it's like Topside. What year is it?"

Adolphine takes in a deep breath. "The year is 1986. There have been two wars, really ..." she says, after a moment, her voice, high, but also thick. "The first came in 1963. Not many records survived the first war, but we've been able to piece together most of the chain of events, especially thanks to

Calvert. Your captain, Amita, was a chaplain in the US Navy, and he, along with an executive officer named Crockett, led a group of about thirty other crewmembers in a mutiny against the captain of this submarine. They felt that war against the Reds..."

"Reds?"

"The Russians ... the enemy of the United States—of America. These two countries were almost at war before, you see ... it was called the Cuban Missile Crisis. Everyone had missiles pointed at each other on the land as well. They thought the Reds were in league with the Devil. That this was the great war, good versus evil. Their mutiny was quick, bloody. Crockett was injured, eventually died from his wounds, but not before he launched all the nukes—except one, which malfunctioned. Calvert was one of those original members."

The elders.

"They forced the rest to join or die—many stayed. Those who didn't were thrown into the sea." She pauses—footsteps crossing above. The grease wick quavers in my hand. When the guard passes, Adolphine continues: "Seems like Crockett's plan was to catch the Reds by surprise. It worked. He hit a number of key air bases and other essential Russian military infrastructure.

"America then had no choice but to follow through with the attack once it began, and for that reason, in the first wave of the war, Russia and the rest of the USSR was hit hardest. America was mostly spared, except for a few cities and bases, while other countries in Europe were in closer range to the SSRs. They soaked up most of the retaliation.

"It was a long war. Two years, it raged on. The Reds weren't down and out—found a way to get a squad of their bombers through. Took out our defenses. Launched the last of their missiles. That's when America got hit good. Starvation followed. Civil unrest. Different factions battled each other, in America, but also in Russia, in Europe. That was pretty much the end of the first war.

"Worst was the radiation poisoning. Most of the people who died in the war died from that."

That I know about. The blue poison.

I see in my mind the Demi, young Bartholomew. A skeleton.

I think of Lazlo.

It doesn't take long for the poison to kill you. To eat you up.

"How many died?" I ask.

Silence again. For a moment.

"No one really knows—estimates are somewhere between one and one and half billion . . . about half the population of the world, some think. Places here in the South Pacific didn't get the worst of it. Japan, the Hawaiian Islands were hit because they were strategic bases . . . but the wind patterns didn't deposit the fallout this far south—and over the years, it dissipated. That's why places like Australia, New Zealand, Malaysia, Papua New Guinea, and Guam survived. That's why I survived."

"What about the second war?"

"After the fall of the American military command, Australia became the center for the fight against the Reds. Though the Russians were worse off than the US, there were still skirmishes between their remaining forces and US forces in the Pacific. The Chinese, meanwhile, had managed to keep out of most of the war until then—they forced the Russians to hand over their remaining tanks and ordnance, and then used them to aggressively absorb countries like Vietnam, Korea, Thailand, and Laos. All under the flag of communism."

"What is a communism?"

"A *communist* is someone with a much different perspective than ours. A system where the people should be the ones who have the power, but, in reality, it's the person in charge who calls the shots. So, in so many ways, it became the same old fight just with different players."

"But you said the other day that peace was at hand," I say.

She pauses. "It is. The Coalition lost the Philippine islands just weeks ago—there was a key base there—to the Eastern Asian Alliance Navy—they call themselves the Liánméng. It won't be long until Australia stands down. Guam will probably do the same." An edge of bitterness. "But the war will be done, finally. Everyone is tired of it."

I hear the exhaustion. The defeat.

"Are your parents alive?" I ask.

This seems to take her off guard. "No. They both died of cancer, a few years ago. They were sent out on rescue missions—trying to move people out of the contaminated zones in Japan. They were exposed."

"I'm sorry."

Poison. Always the poison that kills.

I say, "You mentioned that my parents were probably from Guam—stationed in Guam, like yours. Do . . . do you think you knew my parents? What happened to them?"

"I don't know, Remy," she says, voice bent with sympathy. "I don't think so. If you were taken, then I'm afraid that they may have been killed. Like the others."

I swallow. Wipe my eyes. "I don't know if I believe you and

your people would have spared the brothers on our boat. After all we have done."

"If you had come quietly . . . surrendered . . . then we would have taken you in. I know that for certain. It was Brother Calvert—he made us understand that many of you . . ." She treads carefully here. ". . . have been led to believe lies. For years and years."

"They're after us now," I say, sniffling. "The rest of your people. Hunting us. Suppose I understand that."

"They most likely are," she says. "Depending on how fast this boat is moving, what its bearing is."

"They'll catch us eventually," I say.

"I've heard you singing, haven't I, Remy?" Adolphine speaks to me now the way I would sometimes speak with the younger Choristers—the ones recovering from their cutting, doubled over in pain. "You sing the highest melody."

"Yes."

"It's a . . . beautiful voice. It lifts my spirit."

"That's what Captain Amita always said." I must keep wiping my eyes. "Said that I would be essential. After we launch the missile, then we will dive. We will dive and we will sing into the darkness, and then the years of tribulation will be done. And we will ascend to heaven—"

I say these words, but they are empty to my own ears. Empty of meaning, or faith.

Adolphine doesn't respond at first, but I feel a question coming.

"How . . . how have you managed it?" she asks.

"What?"

"Keeping yourself hidden for so long," she says. Her eyes are wide above me. Gleaming by the dim wicklight.

"I . . . I don't . . ."

"The captain must have helped, didn't he? Someone would have had to. I know what they have done to the little girls they came across. Tossed them into the sea. But they saved you."

I can't breathe. I almost douse the flame in the bilge for my shaking hands.

She knows. I'm found out! What will she do?

"I won't tell anyone, Remy," Adolphine says. Earnestness in her words. "I promise you."

"How . . . how did you know?" I ask.

"Your voice is different than the rest. Not necessarily higher, but cleaner. Clearer. I can hear it," Adolphine says.

"Cap—Captain Amita," I say. "He helped me keep it secret. Said he thought . . . he thought that I was meant to serve a purpose. That's why he spared me."

Adolphine has pressed her fingers through the grating. Only the pads emerge. It's as though she's trying to comfort me. To place a hand on my shoulder. The way Lazlo would.

This, a Topsider. A woman. Meant to be corrupt. But not. No, here she is so very, very human.

"I can't tell anyone the truth about you," I say. "The truth about Topside. Lazlo was sent aft for even telling me."

"Who is Lazlo?"

"He's . . ." I say, trying to find the word for it. But *friend* isn't right. Nor is the term *brother*. "Someone close to me. He was on deck, during the raid. He saw everything that happened to you and your crew. Told me about it. Now he's being punished. Probably will die. Everyone who gets sent to the reactor room dies eventually. The poison."

"I'm . . . sorry, Remy," Adolphine says.

"You should fix the missile," I say, wiping my nose.

"Marston will starve you. He's cruel. Fix the missile so you can eat."

"I cannot do that, child. After I am done, I am dead. Doubt I'd be able to escape. I am weak, and even if I got off this boat, I would be stranded. Even if the Coalition is searching for the *Leviathan*, who knows how far away the closest ship is? No matter what, I die. Most important, I cannot let them launch. I know where the missile is targeted . . ."

"How do you know that?"

"Calvert told us. Australia. Sydney. Millions live there. It's the capital of the southern territories of the Coalition. The last major seat of Western power. There would be no chance for peace after that. It would spark a whole new war . . ."

"It won't launch," I say, clearing my throat. "I have the missile key. Caplain Amita gave it to me. I won't . . . I won't launch it."

6

JUBILATE DEO, OMNIS TERRA; servite Domino in laetitia. Introite in conspectu ejus in exsultatione.

Serve the Lord with gladness. Come before his presence with singing.

I try. I sing, but some ember inside me has dimmed. There is no gladness left in me. I'm not sure if there ever was.

It is None. The ninth hour. The hour when man is most tempted. When Adam and Eve were expelled from the garden.

A watchful hour.

And I feel the weight of so many eyes upon me now. Ex-Oh Goines. Marston. St. John. Especially St. John. He's noted my comings and goings. I'm almost positive he woke up when I last slipped out of my bunk. But if he does suspect something, he hasn't yet informed the caplain. I'm not sure what he's waiting for, but I know I have to be careful.

The reading today is again from Jonah.

"And the sailors said to one another, 'Let's cast lots to discover who is responsible for the calamity that has befallen our ship.' And it was Jonah who was responsible."

Caplain Amita called me his Moses.

But I feel more like Jonah, swallowed up by the Leviathan.

These missile tubes, like the ribs of the beast.

And, like Jonah, I pray now that I might be released, that I be spat onto the shore, alive.

I sing. The hymn, "Eternal Blue Light, My Salvation." One of Captain Amita's.

But I have made a mistake. I realize it now.

I have lost the melody, have been singing half a step lower than the rest of the Choristers and brothers. A sour harmony.

St. John, standing just beside me before the dais, glances my direction. A smirk on his face. I have made his day.

This is not my first mistake this hour. I came in late during the versicle.

Captain Marston has noticed. Standing before us. He raises an eyebrow at me, even though I've corrected. Have slid back up into the proper mode. Have found the motif.

Even so, he calls me up to the control room to meet with him after the hour has ended.

There, I find the captain, along with Ex-Oh and Brother Wasserman, with his stoop, his sallow face lopsided by a massive, purple growth blooming to the left of his nose. Marston is leaning over the large map table, several charts spread out upon it. The topmost one details what seems to be a sea between two large, green-hued landmasses. It is labeled the "Arafura Sea." Not a sea I have heard of.

Amidst that expanse of pale blue sea, speckled with drops of green—isles and archipelagoes—a pencil-marked course has been plotted.

"You have seemed tired of late, Cantor," the captain says, glancing up. He dismisses the others with a wave of his hand, leaving the control room vacant except for Brothers Vicanza and Artemis, who are manning the helm, and Brother Alder, the Watch, at the master control panel.

"Are you feeling well?" Marston asks, stepping around the table, standing between me and the map.

"I see I cannot hide it," I say, mouth very dry. "I have had unrest of late. Sleep has . . . not found me easily."

"A troubled soul?" he asks. His eyes pore over me, as though scouring my face for secrets. My many secrets.

He crosses his arms, leans against the table.

No. If he had found out about my conversations with Adolphine, or about the key, or that I am a girl, then he would not delay in punishing me.

He tilts his head. Even standing a foot from him, it feels as though he is looming over me. Light eyes, flashing bright as ever with conviction. With energy and fervor. "Perhaps it is the fate of young Lazlo that still troubles you?"

Here, I know I should not tell the truth.

"My heart does ache for Lazlo," I say. My words come out tight, as a croak. "I pray for his soul, as you have allowed. But I know there is nothing to be done. He is where he belongs." I say these words as resolutely, as confidently as I can manage. I choke back the anger that has been building in me for days. I can't let on. "I believe I'm just . . . aware of how much responsibility rests upon my shoulders."

This, Caplain Marston seems to believe as genuine. Closes his eyes. Nods heavily. Places a bespotted hand on my shoulder. I fight the urge to cringe, to pull away. "Yes, I see. Of course you would feel it. You should go see Brother Dumas and tell him I have given you permission to take a sleeping nostrum. We need you rested and focused in these last days."

"Very kind, Caplain," I say, bowing my head. "I'm sure that will help me. I won't . . . I won't make any more mistakes."

"Good," he says. "I know you won't. Go on, now."

When he turns to round the desk once more, I see the chart fully—the course plotted in pencil. A location marked with a dot, an X, and scribbled numbers. -9.48, 136.60. Longitude and latitude. Caplain Amita taught me how navigation is done. That these numbers point to an exact location on the globe.

-9.48, 136.60.

I burn them into my mind.

Remember.

"Cantor . . ." the caplain asks.

I've allowed my gaze to linger too long. He's caught me.

"I . . . I always liked looking at maps. Caplain Amita had them in his office. He would show them to me. I always thought they were quite . . . beautiful."

"Indeed," he says. Perhaps wary. Suspicious.

But if he does suspect, he doesn't let on. He dismisses me. I rush from the room before he can say another word.

———————

"I have them. The coordinates," I whisper up into Adolphine's cell.

I waited a full day before coming to visit her again, just to be careful of the caplain's suspicion, and of St. John's ever-vigilant watch of my comings and goings. But today St. John is busy helping Brother Aegis with the mending and sewing of robes, and my job, to inspect the underworks, presents the perfect opportunity.

"What's that, child?" Adolphine asks, her shadowy form appearing on the other side of the grate above.

"I got a look at the chart. The caplain called me up to the control room. We were standing right beside it the whole time."

"Good," Adolphine says, more energetic than I've ever

heard her. "Good girl. Brave girl."

Girl. The word gives me pause. Such weight to it.

There's a bond hidden in this word.

An association so very different than this place. This submarine and everyone on it.

A new covenant.

"Where is the course plotted?" she asks.

"West, to the Arafura Sea," I say.

"Arafura," Adolphine mutters thoughtfully. "A very shallow body of water, between Papua New Guinea and the northern coast of Australia."

"We normally wouldn't sail into such shallow waters," I say. "No room to dive and hide."

"It makes sense. Most of the CPN fleet will still be to the northwest, near the Philippines. They won't be patrolling those waters. Your captain is smart—he's been listening to the radio chatter, figuring out what's been going on up there in the world," she says. "Also, the Polaris missile only has a range of 1300 miles. He would need to get close in order to hit Sydney without sailing into the southern waters around Australia, which will certainly be heavily patrolled. Could you see how close we are to the launch destination? Captains will normally keep track of the boat's position."

"Yes, I saw. There was a solid line that ended with an *X*, and a dotted line continued to the Arafura sea. The X had us just south of an island called Fiji."

"Fiji," Adolphine says, then falls silent.

"What?" I ask.

"Doing the math. I've been aboard ... thirteen ... no, fourteen days. And the *Janus* was attacked just off the coast of the Cook Islands. Means we're only going about ..."

"About 160 miles a day," I answer. "So, we've traveled about two thousand miles."

"That's . . . right. That's right, Remy," she says, the same way she was impressed when I told her I could read words and charts. That Captain Amita taught me. "That's not very fast. Which means we've got about another five or so days . . . yes, five days at least before we reach the launch point. I can stretch out repairs for that long. Brother Ernesto doesn't know much about the electronic systems, the targeting computer, but Goines and your captain do. They know how to check to see if each of the missile and launch systems are in order, that I'm repairing them correctly. No way to fake that. But I'll keep finding ways to delay. Scavenge for parts. That's time."

She seems to be speaking only to herself, thinking out loud.

"Time for what?" I ask.

"For us to send a message . . ." the woman whispers. The whites of her eyes flash in the wicklight.

"Message?"

"Rescue. We're probably too far away for Guam or Australia to receive the transmission, but we're no doubt still being followed by one or two CPN ships. We can send a radio transmission to them. I know the channel to transmit . . . we have a secret code. We can tell them what our launch position will be."

"But they would attack us . . . right? They're hunting us."

"Not if we send them the message that I'm alive. That the missile cannot be launched. Then we surface the boat."

"Caplain Marston would never surrender . . . I told you that . . ."

"We won't get him a choice. We'll disable it," she says, knowingly. "You said you know the *Leviathan* backward and forward, right?"

I think. "Short of taking control of the helm, or the control room . . . and we wouldn't be able to manage that—too many people. We could get to the engine room somehow . . ."

"Exactly," Adolphine says, the way Caplain Amita would offer praise when testing my reading skills.

She says, "We wait until we surface to vent. Then we find a way to shut off engineering from the forward compartments. You said there's only one entry point to access aft, yes?"

"Yes . . . through the tunnel . . ."

"Is it guarded?"

"No—the hatchway is sealed on the forward side. The brothers enter and exit by calling over the squawk. If we're in the middle of a shift, there won't be anyone there."

"Then we could easily get back there and shut off the engine, the generators if we time it right. How many are stationed back there?"

"Two. Two or three brothers at any time."

"That's not many," she says, ever more confident. "Yes, we can take them."

We.

"But . . ." I begin. "I wouldn't want to hurt anyone."

"We won't have to. If we surprise them, we can restrain them. No one has to die."

I think a moment, find myself chewing at a nail. Bitter grease. Most of it pulls away at the quick. Only a little jolt of pain. My fingers no longer have much feeling in them. "But even if we shut off the engine and generators, Marston could still use battery power to dive."

"We disable the hydraulics, then," Adolphine counters. "They won't be able to control the dive planes."

"Then the boat would be dead in the water."

"I know most of the *Leviathan*'s systems," Adolphine says. "I studied them. But I'm not sure if I'd know how to shut everything down. Would you?"

"No," I say. "Lazlo would."

"Yes?"

"Yes, he's very smart. Good with the electrics. With the machines. But even if we could take over the engine room, force the boat to surface, we'd have to send off the message first. How will we get you to the radio room?"

Silence. The boat groans. I feel it shift. Feel the water and seepage flow past my feet. Soon, the hull will resound with the hammer.

"You'll have to do it, Remy," she says.

I swallow.

"But I don't know . . . I don't know how any of it works."

"I can tell you. I can walk you through it—"

"I can't," I say. "I've risked so much already, coming here. I would get caught!" I say, trying to keep control of my voice.

She says, "We could all survive this. You and your friend Lazlo. We have medicines. Treatments."

Topside.

All along, it has been such a distant thought. Sunlight. Air that doesn't reek of oil. Water that doesn't taste bitter, brackish.

What would life look like without the order? Without the ringing of the hull every third hour?

"Others could perhaps help, too," I say. "It will be hard to accomplish this on our own. I could try talking to them . . . to the Forgotten. I could send a message back to Lazlo . . . let him know what to expect."

"And risk getting us caught?" Adolphine asks, her tone suddenly sharp. "Don't do it, Remy. We can't trust others."

"You trust me."

"Yes, but you're the one who came to me, Remy. Can you really say without doubt that you could convince the others to disregard everything they've believed in, everything they've been taught, so quickly?"

I want to fight back. I want to say that I have changed quickly. That my whole world has been turned upside down in a matter of days.

But no . . . it wasn't quick. The cracks were already there, before any of this occurred, before Caplain Amita died. Before I was given the key. I just couldn't see them.

"Do Topsiders believe in God?" I ask.

Adolphine doesn't answer for a few long seconds. "People have always believed in something. Different religions have different names for God. Some believe in many gods."

"Do you believe in God?"

Another pause. "No. I was raised to. My parents believed. But I do not."

"Why?"

"Because . . . I got older and saw what had happened to the world. When I truly realized how many had died, how many continued to suffer—suffering you cannot fathom—I could not imagine a God that would allow such a thing to happen."

"Some of the scripture claims God to be merciful. But some say He is vengeful. Lately, I've had trouble seeing how he could be both."

Adolphine doesn't speak.

"Lazlo doesn't deserve what is happening to him," I say.

"You love him?" she asks, carefully, kindly.

"He's my best friend," I say. "I do . . . I do love him."

I have never said it. *Love* has always been a word associated only with God. But yes.

"We listen to the whales. When we should be sleeping. They sing against the hull. We would listen to them and try to figure out what they were saying to each other. Have you heard them?"

"Yes . . ." she says. "I've heard the whales."

"There's several I can recognize just by their song. Now I only hear one."

Silence.

The creaking of the boat. Footsteps somewhere. A compressor hisses in the next compartment.

"We can save him, Remy," Adolphine whispers from above, voice full of light. Of hope. "We can save them all. And ourselves."

———

I find Brother Callum alone at his nightly station, manning the radio room on the main level. The *Leviathan* often tows a buoy with an antenna cable in order to listen to the Topside transmissions, even from great depths. But, especially on nights like this, when we surface in order to vent gasses, the station must be manned. To scan for our enemies. For prey.

He is focused, ears covered by the bulky headset. He starts upon turning to find me standing at the hatchway, his one uncovered grey eye wide. He looks cross, ready to scold, but softens upon seeing what I've brought. A bowl full of steaming ginger steep.

I must continue adjusting it in my hands to keep it from spilling.

The boat sways, pitches heavily. It creaks and groans. It's a rocking, stormy sea out there tonight. Normally, the *Leviathan* would dive deep beneath the squalls, but on venting nights, there is no choice.

Brother Callum, normally red-faced, has a sallow and green countenance. He does not handle bad weather well.

And so, he accepts the steep gratefully, waving me inside, keeping one hand braced against the broad console.

The radio room is small—just big enough to hold two seats positioned before a vast, bulky array of electronic equipment. A face of switches and dials and knobs that fill an entire wall of the compartment. I take the empty seat next to him.

I see exactly the electronic equipment I am to use. The tuner, where I am to change the broadcast channel. The tele-type machine, in the corner, likely unused since the days leading up to the war.

Will it still work?

I shouldn't be in here. No Chorister should, but Brother Callum, normally one of the most observant, one of the strictest in our order, has softened since Silas's death. Not just to me but to Ephraim and Caleb, and even St. John, who tends to stoke the ire in most people.

The overall mood on the boat has been muted since Silas's death.

They were close.

"Do you hear the enemy?" I whisper.

"There's nothing out there. Not in this storm," he says, taking a long sip of the steep. A particularly large swell rocks the compartment upward, pitches him so that he almost spills the bowl.

He mutters, closes his eyes, takes another long draw.

Silence has always meant something different in Brother

Callum's presence. He clearly was never inclined to be a loquacious person, and so has always seemed to abide the mandate of our order, our silence, with greater ease than the other brothers. Perfectly happy in it.

Not tonight.

Tonight, he is discontented.

He takes another sip. Closes his eyes.

Too soon, I think. *Too soon for the nostrum to take effect.*

Even though it is a powerful treatment. Caplain Amita often took it, in his last days, to stave off pain long enough to find some rest.

Here, I have used all three doses' worth.

Not enough to harm someone.

I asked Brother Dumas what would happen if I took all the powder at once.

He laughed and simply said it would be a long, uninterrupted sleep. That I would certainly be unable to rise for the call to Matins.

So, I would not hurt anyone. Yet I feel guilty for doing it.

"He liked you, you know?" Brother Callum says.

"Who?"

"Brother Silas," he says, clearing his throat.

I almost don't know what to say. "I . . . I liked him as well."

"We was rescued real close together, you know?" he asks. He doesn't intend for me to answer. "Silas and me. We was both of us a few weeks apart, coming here. I was on a boat with my parents. Refugees. I was ten."

Brother Callum has slumped in his seat. No, this is not the nostrum. This is something else. I can do nothing but listen as he continues:

"My parents and I lived in Hawaii. Civilians. Not military, I mean. When the big island got hit, us and a few other families got together on this . . . yacht. That's a sailboat. Not very big. Not big for all of us, for sure. We were eight, total. Sailing for New Zealand. Dad thought that would be the best place to ride out the rest of the war. That was the plan. All the way across the Pacific. Food ran out, though. Mom got sick. Not sure what it was, but whatever it was, killed three out of the eight of us. Then we ran out of water. No rain for a bad, hot stretch. Out of food. One of my friends' parents. Man named Ellison. Went nuts. Killed my father—intended to eat him and me, but I stood up to him. Killed him. Knocked him across the back of the head with an oar. Then I guess I was in charge. I knew how to sail well enough. But then the heat and the thirst really got most of us. It was just me and a girl in the end. Daughter of one of the friends. Girl named Moira. She was about . . . eight, I guess. Eight. Boat was in bad shape—we'd gotten battered by a typhoon. Knocked out our mast. We were drifting then. We weren't going to make it another day or two when we came upon this small island. Saw the *Leviathan* out, just past the shoals. Surfaced. Thought we were saved. I was, well enough. Caplain Amita, he was a good man, took me in. Said that Moira couldn't come, though. That there were too many mouths. That we were doing God's work, yeah. No women. No women allowed in the garden. I couldn't really sing—but I was strong for my age. I had purpose. Survived my cutting. My purification. Moira, though. We left her, yeah. On that island. Only a few palms. Probably no fresh water. I re-member I . . . didn't even fight to bring her on board. Maybe I could have begged the caplain, changed everything, but I didn't. Felt damn lucky to just be alive, suppose. To have pur-pose. And we left her. Yeah, we did. And she probably died there. On the island. Might not've. But probably, yeah. Probably still there." He grunts, staring down at the last slurp of steep in the bowl before taking it down in a final swig.

His eyelids have grown heavier, but he shows no sign of stopping, of not talking. I look out the door, peek either way down the hall outside to see if anyone is in earshot. But Brother Callum seems not to care. He continues:

"That's how you were rescued, you know . . . from a boat, adrift at sea. Skin blistered and salt-cracked when we found you—I remember. Skinny little thing. Didn't think you would survive. Caplain took a liking to you, all right. Good thing, because Marston would have just left you there. But Caplain nursed you back to health hisself. A good man, in all. Harsh, but good. Said you were special. An' he was right about that, wasn't he?"

"I . . . I suppose," I say, not knowing how to respond.

I remember the burn of the sun behind my eyelids, just now. A flash of blinding light bursting through layers and buried memory. The feel of it. The dry, salty, stinging lips.

"Was I alone?" I ask. "When I was found?"

Brother Callum blinks slowly, groggily. "You know, I don't remember."

He gives half a colorless laugh.

"Remember when I first heard you sing, yeah. All of us knew . . . we knew you were special. Knew God had spared you for a reason. Silas loved it. Loved hearing your voice. Said it sounded like an angel."

His eye is welling up now. Red, and angry.

"Here, I want you to listen to something," he says suddenly, pulling one side of the headset on his ear while turning the tuning knob on the console, clearly searching for something.

"Listen?"

"It'll all be over soon, won't it?" he asks, words thick now, whispering. "It won't matter. I want you to hear something. Sometimes I listen. Something just for me. Ah, this is a good one . . ." He smiles, his mouth slack. Before I can respond, he has removed the headset from around his neck and is placing them over my ears.

The creaking of the boat, the squeal and the whine of distressed metal disappear in a sea of crackling, popping static. Harsh. Loud. I want to pull it off. Then I hear it. Swimming somewhere behind the static

Music. Music without voices. Rhythm. Cracks. Instruments that blare, lurking behind a curtain of static that pitches and wails and sometimes swallows but does not fully obscure.

Where is the voice? I think.

And then she enters—a melody, sung not in English. In some other beautiful language—a voice that seems to be moving in hot, short notes.

Energy. Life. Being transmitted out from some island, from some city, where people live and walk and breathe the free air. Something indescribably happy that pours into me. Pours in through my ears, into my heart.

When have I ever felt so light?

"What is it called?" I ask.

But Brother Callum is already fast asleep, still seated in his chair, head slumped.

I don't want this to end—this music—but I must. There is no time. I can't risk being caught.

I pull the headphones off and turn the same big knob on the massive console Brother Callum was adjusting only moments before until the needle on the dial rests at the appropriate wavelength. I follow the instructions Adolphine went over in detail. Next, I pull away a plastic cover from the teletype machine to reveal an array of dusty, grey-colored keys. I toggle the power switch and wait. The machine hums gently as the green indicator light slowly winks to life. *Still works.*

I take the slip of parchment tucked in my bindings and quickly begin to punch in the series of letters and numbers scratched on one of the pieces of parchment Caplain Amita gave me years ago for practicing my letters.

A coded message detailing the *Leviathan's* launch destination and instructions for how to approach.

It's a noisy business. Each imprinted key causes a sharp snapping sound to emanate from the machine when I press it. Thankfully, the *Leviathan* is loud tonight, groaning metal and clangs and knocks with every swell and dip. Brother Callum remains slumped in his seat, in a deep slumber. After I have quickly, carefully punched in the sequence, I find the orange TRANSMIT key just where Adolphine said it would be. I strike it.

And with a muted ticking, the message is sent into the world. And perhaps our salvation. A way for us all to survive.

To not drown in these icy depths.

I look over to find Brother Callum slumped in the exact same position, snoring softly. He'll get in trouble if he's found sleeping on his watch. But not as much trouble as he would get in if Ex-Oh Goines found me in here with him.

Quietly as I can, I stand, I turn the tuning dial back to the channel he had been scanning when I first came in. Switch off the teletype machine, covering it.

I'm about to leave when I hear the crackling voice speaking through the headphones.

I should leave now. The corridor is empty. No one will see me slip out. But the temptation is too great.

I put one side of the headset over my ear.

It's a man speaking. English. Though, the reception is especially fuzzy. More so than the channel that was broadcasting the music.

"—ations are underway for Prime Minister Aldeway . . . formally surrender CPN forces to . . . Liánméng navy after the utter defeat of the . . . tion fleet in the battle for Subic Bay . . . not yet clear whether the Northern Protectorate . . . comply with Minister Aldeway's plea for peace . . . end to war. Word has not yet come from Guam . . ."

The report is swallowed, disappears in the din.

When I remove the headset, I hear a sharp intake of breath from behind me.

There, standing just outside the half-opened door, Ephraim. Lips drawn tight. Expression inscrutable.

7

"CAN WE TRADE TEETH?" Caleb asks, placing his spoon down beside his mess kit.

"Why bother?" St. John asks. "We surely only have days left before we deliver the Last Judgment. What good will such earthly goods be to us?"

Caleb falls silent, looks down to his murky broth.

"You need not sour his spirits so," I say. "He's scared."

"He should be rejoicing," St. John says, that haughty, superior tone. "At last, our service will be rewarded."

"Regardless," I say, unable to keep quiet, looking at Caleb's pale face. "It might be a . . . frightening time to some."

Ephraim glances up at me. Normally, he would step in, particularly when Caleb is involved.

I tried reasoning with Ephraim after he found me in the radio room, hooking him by the arm before he could scurry off down the corridor.

"It was nothing," I told him.

But he wouldn't look at me. As though I was diseased, as though, just by proximity, he himself was damned.

How much had he seen?

"I was listening to music," I said. "I had never listened before. And Brother Callum fell asleep . . ."

"Remy . . ." he said, pulling his arm away. "I don't know what you're up to. . . . I don't want to know . . . but St. John does. And if he finds out, you'll be . . . you'll be in *so* much trouble. You know Caplain Marston . . . and if he finds out I knew and didn't say anything . . ."

"I won't get caught. And even if I did, the caplain won't find out about you. Not from me," I said, laying a hand at the center of his chest. "Promise."

He swallowed. Finally, he looked up. Such young eyes, fearful eyes, even though he is at least three years older than me. I'd never noticed before then.

His whole body shook.

"Do you trust me?" I asked him.

And he nodded, taking in a breath.

"Things are happening. About to happen. I can't tell you any more than that. Just . . . please keep trusting me. Please?"

He nodded again.

But he has remained cool toward me, even two days later. Not glancing up, and speaking little, if at all, during meals. Our usual silence punctuated somehow by a greater silence.

St. John has noticed. Of course he has.

He grins into his bowl. I can almost see the acerbic retort taking shape in his mind.

"You've been quiet, Ephraim," St. John says. "I know Remy must be so tired from his nightly excursions—but you are normally not so staid."

That grin. Sly. Devious.

I set down my spoon.

Ephraim's eyes go wide.

St. John says, "I thought Caplain Marston was as . . . taken with you as old Caplain Amita, but that isn't the case after all."

He leaves no room for response.

"When I told him about Lazlo, about what I heard you two

talking about in the balneary, he was taken aback. Dangerous ideas, Remy. I confessed to the caplain that I did fear dear Lazlo had . . . already corrupted your soul. He asked me to keep a close watch on you. To search for the signs of corruption."

I fight the urge to jump across the table, to wipe the smirk from St. John's face. I fight it with all my being.

"You two should take heed," St. John says, nodding to Ephraim and Caleb, both of whom have been watching in tense silence. "After all, look at poor Lazlo . . . look where his association with Remy got him."

How much does St. John know?

"Please, you don't care anything about their souls," I say. "You just care about position. You only removed Lazlo because you don't have half his talent."

"Jealous of that little worm," he snaps, sitting up straight. Gives a fake, shrill laugh. But I know I've struck a nerve. I shouldn't be risking an altercation. Shouldn't risk being found out. Not so close to our final days. But I can't help myself.

"Envious of his voice—of his position. And mine as well," I say.

This does it.

He springs to his feet. Everyone in the mess has fallen silent. All eyes on St. John. "What I care about are the rules . . . and you've got away with breaking them too long. You think you're special. That you're above them. But you aren't. I know Caplain agrees. Better keep your eyes about you, yeah? *Because I think you've got a secret . . . and I'm going to find it out!*"

He whispers these last, fuming words, but they are still loud enough for all in earshot to hear.

Now I'm the one who stands. The table remains between us. Everyone watching.

"*Remy,*" Ephraim whispers, nervous.

I brace myself, ready to fight if I need to. Ready to throw a fist, until the compartment pitches suddenly downward.

I must latch on to Ephraim's arm to keep my balance..

We are diving. Fast.

The red bulb on the bulkhead above the hatchway begins flashing. No alarm. A flashing light means we are running silent.

"We're being hunted," Ephraim whispers.

Brother Aegis slides down the ladder from the main deck, rushing aft, toward the chapel. Brother Dumas follows.

"What's going on?" St. John asks.

"Enemy vessel," he grunts with urgency. "Think it might be a sub."

"I thought all the subs were destroyed," Caleb says.

"That's what I heard Ex-Oh Goines say," Brother Aegis says, bracing himself against the bulkhead as the downward pitch grows steeper. Ephraim and I must do the same, to keep our balance. St. John and Caleb cling onto the table as dishes and cutlery spill to the deck in an enormous clang and clatter.

"What are you waiting for? All to their stations!" the brother commands, breaking all from our stupor. The mess erupts in a quick scramble—each of the brothers rushing away. Brother Dumas has ordered Ephraim to help Brother Ernesto secure the air system. St. John is sent to the lower deck of the chapel, to check for leaks.

Then a screaming, metallic shrieking wails past the hull. A few seconds later, an explosion. The deck lurches out from beneath me. I lose my legs. Am slammed hard onto the deck face-first, rolling, sliding down the steep decline, coming to a painful stop as my shoulder jams into the forward bulkhead.

Electric pain lances down my arm. Breath knocked from my lungs. Taste blood. Squiggly points of light dance before my eyes. I feel my forehead. My fingers are slick.

It's Ephraim who lifts me up. When the ringing in my ears stops, I hear spraying water. Smell acrid fume.

He says words that I can't seem to hear. Not at first. I read his lips.

"The pumps. Take Caleb with you!"

I nod, am already breaking away, running up the tilt, despite my blurry vision, my uncertain feet. I move against the flow of the other brothers darting to their stations. I find Caleb hiding beneath one of the tables, clinging to one of the bolted-down legs.

The pitch of the deck has leveled somewhat. Easier to walk.

I snatch up his hand and drag him along with me.

One of the mains just above us has burst, jetting a torrent of water into the compartment. Brother Aaron is already trying to patch it.

Another passing shriek in the water outside the hull. A muffled explosion, much farther away than the last. The *Leviathan* still resonates. Rattles. Groans.

Not depth charges. These must be torpedoes. I've never actually heard them before. The *Leviathan*'s stockpile was used up long before I was brought on board.

"Caleb, stick with me!" I shout over the roar of the water, the shouting, the thrum and knock of pressure against the hull.

Jumping down into the well, there's barely room to move around the massive bank of batteries. The water has already pooled here to my ankles. I help Caleb down.

"There are two pumps—I need you to turn this one, back here." I point to the pump handle aft, away from the water pooling at the forward part of the well. The motorized pumps burned out long ago, and they must be manually operated in order to clear the water through the bilge.

I glance to the metal strut, just above where Caleb has started pumping, to where I hid the missile key. No time to check on it now.

I inch around the side of the battery bank, forward to the other manual pump release. The water is deeper here—ever deepening. To my knees. We're still diving. Leakage continues to spill in from the hatch above in a waterfall, dousing the batteries.

They're made to handle being wet and not shorting out, but they can't become submerged. If they do, they'll fry. The batteries would be dead, and so would Caleb and I. Electric shock.

Another screech from the deck above—the sound of the trim main blowing. The water cascades down now, drenching me.

It's already up to my waist when my fingers find the pump handle, just beneath the murky, salty, greasy surface. I begin working it, spinning the wheel valve.

Shouting. The clanging of feet scurrying on the decks above. The rushing of water. More and more spilling in. The *Leviathan* is still diving. Still dropping fast. I hear the entire boat groan from the pressure. We're going to reach the crush depth soon at this rate of descent.

There might be a war raging on the upper decks, but here is the only thing that matters.

Turn, turn, turn.

The pump isn't draining the water away fast enough. We're barely keeping up.

"Caleb, I need you to speed up!" I shout.

I can't see him around the battery cluster behind me, but I hear him. Hear him grunting as he turns his pump. I also see the bottom bank is already about to be fully submerged.

Not worth risking both our lives.

"Caleb, climb out," I shout.

"But the water—" I hear him shout.

"Do it now. Find the tool kit. I'll call down for something if I need it. Just stay up there!"

The water level continues to rise, but Caleb does as I instructed. I look up to see his legs disappearing through the hatch above.

Meanwhile, I spin and spin the pump valve. I'm dizzy. My eyes burn from the acrid fume. My lungs ache. I'm choking. My arm is numb, but I keep at it.

And then the whole boat lurches, wrenches, *thongs* like I've never heard it before.

My head knocks against the ceiling of the low compartment.

It's as though the whole boat has struck something.

Have we bottomed out? I can't tell if the boat is still moving. It certainly isn't diving any longer.

The lights flicker overhead, then wink out completely. The main power has shut down. Battery power now, keeping the auxiliary lights on.

Without main power, the batteries are essential until the reactor and the generators are brought back online.

I must keep at it.

Thankfully, the burst main seems to have been repaired. The cascade of water has lessened to a small stream pouring in through the well hatch. The boat has also leveled, shifting the water back from where it had been pooling.

There's light enough to see that the pumping might finally be working. The bilge is beginning to recede.

I turn and turn not stopping until the water level has fallen below my ankles. My burning arm quakes, muscles clenching, angry and taut.

But the batteries are safe.

"Caleb, what's going on up there?" I ask, panting.

No answer. Probably still looking for the tool kit. Or hiding under the table again.

I look over to the beam where I've hidden the missile key.

I feel for the key in the small crevice between the ceiling and the top of the beam, where I had carefully had wedged it. But I find only empty space.

I search again, running my fingers along the entire seam, but no. Nothing. No key.

It must have fallen into the water.

"Remy," someone calls from above.

"A moment," I say, coughing, splashing in the cold, murky water, feeling around the bottom.

If I've lost it, then that changes everything.

My fingers probe the rusty metal compartment deck, brush against sharp metal corroded edges.

"Remy!" I hear my name again. It's Ephraim calling down.

Come on!

And then I find it. The smooth metal stalk. The key. Not sucked into the pump, after all.

Now is not the time to take a moment of relief. I shake as I tuck the key safely beneath my wet bindings, where I feel its cold shape pressing into my skin. Where it will stay for the next several days. Should we actually survive long enough to go through with the plan.

I finally climb up from the well, robes sopping wet, heavy.

It isn't until I'm on deck that I recognize the silence that has overtaken the vessel. A hissing, a dripping, a tapping somewhere in the pipes, but quiet otherwise.

A thick haze of oily and electric smoke hangs about the dim compartment. Worse here than below. My eyes burn. My legs tell me that we must have bottomed out. We are resting at a slight tilt.

In the hazy darkness, I make my way forward until I see Ephraim's form, leaning over something on the deck.

"What's going on?"

Ephraim turns—face twisted up in sorrow.

I see now that he's bent over a small, crumpled body. Only leaning in close do I see familiar, childish features half-obscured by a mass of dark gore.

Caleb.

"Wh—what happened?" I ask.

"Pipe must have come loose when we struck bottom," he says, smudging his cheeks with dirty hands. Sniffling. "Thought he was down in the well with you."

"He was," I say, trying to blink away the burning. "I sent him out. Thought it would be safer."

Now is the hour of Vespers, one of the most important prayers of the day. The prayer before a feast. The longest in the liturgy.

It is a time of sacrifice. Of giving back to God.

He had his offering today. Little Caleb.

Normally, I would sing the Magnificat during this hour. The Canticle of the Virgin Mary.

Fecit potentiam in brachio suo;
Dispersit superbos mente cordis sui.
Deposuit potentes de sede, et exaltavit humiles.
Esurientes implevit bonis, et divites dimisit inanes.
Sicut erat in principio, et nunc, et semper, et in saecula saeculo-
    rum. Amen.

He hath put down the mighty from their seat: and hath ex-
    alted the humble and meek.
He hath filled the hungry with good things: and the rich he
    hath sent empty away.
As it was in the beginning, is now, and ever shall be: world
    without end. Amen.

But the Sunset Office is not met tonight. Unessential crew has been ordered to their bunks. No excessive movement or activity. We must keep the air consumption down, while we are still submerged. Hiding, grounded, on the sea floor. Two hundred and nineteen fathoms.

Caleb's body is in the balneary, awaiting its final rights. We cannot commit his body to the deep until the threat is gone.

The sub must still be up there, hunting for us.

It has been a full day.

The reactor and electric generators have been brought back online, but the air is running out. The oxygen generator must have been damaged. The rest of the scrubbers must have shut down.

My throat burns.

Every breath is tight. Each gasp filled with smoke and oil fume and poison.

The berthing compartment is full with my fellow brothers, sleeping or trying to sleep, or gasping for breath in their bunks.

But I'm listening. Ear to the hull. Listening to that lonely strain reaching through the depths.

One whale is singing. Yes, just one.

"*What are you looking for, Brother Whale?*" I whisper. "*Your friend? Has he been taken from you? Your family? Were they put somewhere far away? Is there a deep dark even too deep for you?*"

It is a sad song. I hear the bend, the strain. I sing softly with it, with broken voice. I follow its odd, unearthly melody. My voice wants to sing with it, to let it teach me.

A song of mourning for little Caleb. For all of us.

I wonder if Lazlo has been injured in this attack. And what of Adolphine?

It strikes me that now might just be the best time to check on her, when all are silent.

———

"It was the Liánméng," Adolphine whispers weakly through the grate. "Would recognize the scream of their torpedoes anywhere. The Chinese have been using old Soviet ordnance since the end of the war. They might have intercepted our transmission."

"I thought you said it was a code I was transmitting . . . a secret code."

"Even if they couldn't read the code, they could have triangulated our position. But yes . . . they may have cracked it."

"Then Caleb's death is my fault . . ."

"Caleb?" She asks. I hear her every breath. Strained, like mine.

"A Chorister. Like me. Killed during the attack. He was . . . very young," I say.

"I'm sorry," Adolphine says. "It wasn't your fault. It's my fault."

I swallow, take in a slow breath. "I'm beginning to think . . . in trying to survive, we might accidentally kill more people. That sub might be waiting for us at the coordinates I transmitted. Waiting to destroy us . . ."

"We can't know, Remy . . ."

"Why would they be after us in the first place?"

"They've been hunting you for years. This boat is a threat to either side. Plus, they might want what you have."

"The Last Judgment?"

Her silence confirms it.

"Why?" I ask.

"There aren't any nukes left. Not after the wars. At least, none that aren't sitting in irradiated territories. It would be a commodity—" She stifles a cough. "A way to secure their power. We'll be sailing into Australian waters soon," she says thoughtfully. "They might not follow, risk causing an incident with the ceasefire . . ."

"I heard . . . on the radio, when I sent the message," I say. "Australia will officially surrender in a few days. They said they weren't sure about Guam."

No word for a moment. "Peace, then."

She should sound happier than she does. "Isn't that a good thing?" I ask. "Isn't that what the world has been waiting for?"

"Yes, of course. But peace on equal terms. If Australia gives in, rolls over, then the Liánméng will be the world's superpower. Communists." She coughs again. "This air tastes bad."

"We'll have to surface soon," I say.

"It won't be soon enough. This CO_2 buildup is getting poisonous," she says. I think she must be lying down, by the sleepiness in her voice.

"I think I should get rid of the key," I say, feeling the hard metal pressing into my chest. "As long as I have it, the caplain could still get his hands on it."

"No," she says sharply. "No, don't do that."

"But even if we survive until we get to the launch location, what if our plan fails?" I ask. "What if we can't take the engine room?"

"Then you keep it in order to trade your life for it."

Or Lazlo's.

"It's more valuable than you, than me, than anyone else to Marston. Let him launch."

"But . . . what about Sydney?" I ask.

"I've almost fixed the missile—it will launch, but I've found a way to reprogram the targeting computer. Even if Marston does get the key, the missile will launch into the sea. The middle of nowhere. Where it can't hurt anyone. No, that key is power, Remy. You keep it. Don't let anything happen to it until we're safely off this boat."

"Assuming we survive this—that we make it to the Arafura Sea, and the enemy hasn't tracked us . . ."

Silence. No comforting word.

"Do you think the Coalition will be there? That they even heard us?" I ask.

"They received the message," Adolphine says. "But they might not make it in time. Might not be any ships in the area. Should be two days until we reach it now. Maybe three, once we're under way again."

"I heard Brother Roberts say we're just west of New Caledonia."

"Okay, that's two days away from our launch location, based on the *Leviathan*'s pace."

Two.

Two more days.

"Remy," Adolphine says, her tone one of caution now. "If the plan doesn't work, like you said . . . if we can't force the boat to surface, I'd like for you to promise me that you'll try to escape. Regardless."

"How . . ."

"If we're close enough to the surface, you can ditch . . . escape through the trunk. Did you ever train on that? Most submariners have."

"No. But . . . Brother Calvert told me about it."

Ditching. Swimming out from the cold depths. That darkness. It puts a chill in me, just thinking about it.

"But it won't come to that," I say.

"Like you said, we might not be able to take the engine room, or something . . . something might just go wrong. Just . . . survive, okay, Remy? Try."

Her tone makes me feel worse, not better.

"Promise me?" Adolphine presses.

"Okay . . . I promise. But I'm not going without Lazlo . . ."

"Look out for *yourself*, girl!" Adolphine hisses, almost angry. "Would he risk his life for you?"

"I know he would," I respond, equally as sharp.

This silences her for a time. I hear her labored breathing.

"I'm sorry," she finally says. "I am tired. They aren't letting me sleep."

"I . . . I understand."

The boat groans suddenly. The bilge water sloshes past my feet, toward aft.

"We're rising," I whisper, heart lurching.

"Thank goodness," Adolphine sighs. "Air."

"I should go. I'll try to come back soon," I say. "But I think I'm being watched . . ."

"Then don't risk it. Follow the plan. You'll know when it's time to come for me. When we surface again. When we arrive at the launch location. Two days."

"Yes, two days," I say, my hand reaching for the hard piece of metal still tucked in my bindings, pressed against my chest.

———————

Between my own collection, and Lazlo's and Caleb's, I count forty-six teeth in total, spread out on my bunk. Molars and eye teeth and incisors. Some yellowed, some pipped, but most clean, cream-colored. I wonder if anyone else has gathered so many. I sweep them into a darned wool sock, and, by wick-light, when others are bunked down for second sleep, I write my message with lampblack ink on the very last of the sheaves of scrap parchment Caplain Amita gave to me.

Lazlo,

You were right. About everything. Caplain will try to launch the Last Judgment soon, but we have a plan to stop it. We will need your help. In two days, be ready.

I hesitate a moment over the next words. Only a moment.

I love you,
R.

Simple. I can't give away too much. Almost none of the younger brothers can read, but should an elder get hold of it, at least they won't know too much of the plan.

If found, I would certainly be in trouble. Marston would know that it was I sending the message.

Yet, no matter the risk, no matter what Adolphine says, it's important that Lazlo know something of what is about to happen. She doesn't trust him. She doesn't know him.

I do.

After the afternoon meal, I find Brother Dormer heading to the fan room. That's where I corner him, when St. John and the other brothers are nowhere to be seen.

He's about to protest, when his eyes widen at the pouch I'm carrying.

Even more surprised when I place it directly into his large hands.

He bounces it, hears the rattle.

In the speechlessness that follows, I lean in.

"Inside is something I need for you to give to Lazlo. A folded-up bit of parchment. Don't let anyone else see it. Don't talk about it with anyone. Just give it to him."

Brother Dormer looks positively torn—such a bounty in his palm. He opens the sock and begins to inspect. "I couldn't . . ."

He stammers.

I see images of extra helpings of stew, of sweet cake, should there ever be sweet cake again, swim in his eyes. "What does it say?" he asks. "This message."

"It says that I hope he is okay . . . that I miss him," I say.

He nods, silently, weighing the teeth in his hand against his morality.

"Just make sure he gets it, and I'll give you any teeth I get traded for as long as I live," I say.

He cracks half a smile. Less teeth than anyone on board, Brother Dormer. Black gaps broken with yellow and brown borders. "We in't going to be living that much longer, yeah?"

His voice carries no humor. If anything, it is fear. Uncertainty, at least. The same uncertainty that presses down upon all of us.

Perhaps it's that we survived the last attack when so many thought we wouldn't.

Some stroke of real humanity, coursing through all of us.

"Right," I say.

He nods, solemnly, bounces the tied sock full of teeth in his palm again.

"Okay," he whispers. "I'll do it."

I nod. Take a breath. "Thank you, Brother."

He doesn't know how to react when I embrace him, wrap my arms around his middle.

"He doesn't look . . . good, you know," he says before I take my leave. "Lazlo. He isn't well. Looks sick. He's sick like the others get when they work in the reactor compartment."

My heart drops. I try not to show it. I can't, lest I look too suspicious. "Just give him the message. Please."

I can't breathe, even though the boat has surfaced and vented, and even though Brother Ernesto got the oxygen generator operating again.

The sensation lasts throughout the whole day—me, singing, trying to take a deep breath, but it's as though my bindings are made of iron chains, keeping me from taking in a proper breath. My voice comes out weak, strained. If anyone notices, and I'm sure they do, they say nothing to me about it.

It's not until just after Vespers the next day, when I find the moment to break away, informing Brother Ernesto that I am going to check on the pumps in the battery room.

As soon as I climb down, I remove my robes, still damp and reeking from the attack the day before. Then I unwrap myself, release my chest from the itchy bindings. Take in a deep breath.

Cry.

I let myself, key in my hand.

My shoulder aches from being jarred when the sub bottomed out. My head throbs where it struck the beam.

Only one more day.

One more.

There might still be time to save Lazlo. The radiation might not have gotten to him yet. It might just work. This dangerous, insane plan.

And then, Topside. Sunlight. Fresh air.

"Who would have imagined?" a cold voice calls out. "Here, at our final hour, I find our brave Cantor, so broken . . ."

I whip around to find that St. John has followed me down into the battery well. I didn't even hear him.

He seems about to continue with whatever biting words he had begun when he sees the silver key in my hand.

Confusion. But then his eyes widen. And that wide gaze falls upon me, upon my chest. I close my robes, but it's too late.

He's seen.

The light of realization dawning on his face, fallen heavy as a hammer.

The smirk disappears. In its wake, shock.

Not now. Not so soon! Not when everything is at stake.

"St. John," I say, trying to find the words.

His confusion bends quickly to a fierce, cold malice.

"What secrets you've been keeping, Remy," he says.

He's closed the distance between us in a few steps, snatching the key from my hand before I can even react.

"Give it back," I say, reaching for it.

"And what is this?" he demands, gripping it tight, dodging my darting hand. "Something you stole from the caplain . . . like the sinner you are . . . like the impure creature that was cast from the garden . . ."

"Not stolen," I say, angry now. "Given to me. Entrusted to me. By Caplain Amita."

"Lies! Tell me what it is. What does it open?" he demands.

"It's . . . it's the key that will launch the Last Judgment," I blurt out. It might be the only way to convince him. Or at least, it might surprise him. Take him off his guard. "Caplain Amita entrusted it to me."

St. John's mouth grows slack. He squints down at the key. Confused. Disbelieving.

"The key? To the Last Judgment? He . . . he gave it to a . . . to a female?" he says, almost hissing. "You bewitched him. You've bewitched us all . . ."

"He knew all along," I say.

"Lies." His eyes positively glow. "How Caplain Marston will reward me . . ."

"Give it back," I warn.

"I don't think so . . ." he says, beginning to back away. "No, you'll swim for this, Remy. For this deception."

I lunge forward but am met with the hard back of St. John's hand across the cheek. I'm knocked to the deck, stunned.

He turns, already climbing up from the well, but I push myself up, lunge for his legs, yanking him down. He topples hard against the bank of batteries. Rolls off, down to the deck. I am atop him before he can spring to his feet. Even though I am slighter than he, he cannot push me away. No matter how much he thrashes, struggles.

I think of all he has done. What he did to Lazlo.

I bring my fist across his face.

And again, with my other fist—more vicious, stronger than I intended. The wet smack. Tears bead hot on my cheeks, down my chin. I can barely see him for the tears. I sling my other fist at him, and then again, each blow stronger than the last. My knuckles sting. They ache. Lazlo's face swirls in my mind. With it, a white-hot rage. It is this bastard's fault that Lazlo is back there, dying. It is all St. John's fault. His nose spouts blood.

Finally, I stop myself and look down at him, almost as dazed as he. Tears stream down the sides of his face. He tries to roll me from atop him, weakly, one last time, but I pin him down by the shoulders with all my might.

"*You're wrong. About everything,*" I say through gritted teeth. "*We've been wrong all along!*"

I'm not sure if he even hears me. His eyes are open, but it is as though he's blinking away a fog. I take the key from his loosened grip.

Then, with all the strength left in me, I flip him around and, using a length of rope from the tool kit, I bind his hands, his feet. Stuff some of my binding linens into his mouth. Then I drag him to the far corner of the compartment, so that he won't be seen from the hatch.

Looking down upon him, at what I've done, I gasp. My blood goes cold as the sea.

There's no choice now. Nothing to be done. We have to act. A day early. We have to act now.

I go first to my bunk, to gather my small cache of victuals I've been able to stash away. A few bits of dried fish. Sour grey cake. Next, I must journey through the mess hall, past the elders' wardroom in order to access the lower level of the chapel, where Adolphine is being kept. The mess is abuzz with activity. On the tables, bolts of fresh cloth have been unrolled—they must have been brought on board from the raid on Adolphine's ship. Or kept in storage. New white robes are being sewn for all. Our final dive is coming soon.

I nod to those brothers who greet me, keep my eyes down. My bloodied knuckles, just barely hidden beneath the cuff of my robes.

No one will notice St. John is missing until well after the hour.

A few minutes. That's all I need.

Further down the corridor, I peek through the hatchway into the chapel. Several brothers are congregated around the missile diagnostic panel with Brother Ernesto, just a few feet from Adolphine's cell.

There's no way I'll be able to release her without being caught.

I couldn't have chosen a worse time to set our plan into motion.

But I also can't wait.

I'll go to engineering first, then. Will go to Lazlo.

That's the better plan, anyway, to give him time to figure out how to shut down the engine and hydraulics. Everything must happen fast if this is going to work.

I'll come back to release Adolphine when the rest of the plan is in motion.

The auxiliary machine compartment is abandoned. No one sees me wheel open the hatch and pass through the tunnel, crossing a threshold I have never dared before now.

And so easy.

The first compartment through the tunnel is the aft machine room—a dim space, filled with the familiar blockish shapes of banks of corroded batteries. Generators. Secondary and backup systems for the boat.

The maneuvering shack is in the next compartment back, on the other side of the banks of generators. That's where the reactor and engine functions are controlled. There, Brother Leighton will be on duty. Best to steer clear. Instead, I take the first ladder to the lowest level of engineering and find myself in what must be the main engine room. A great, long machine fills the low, narrow space, its two rows of pistons pumping in a rhythmic, deafening metallic concert. That thrum and rhythm I have known so well, now deafening, so close to the source.

I turn to find myself standing in front of what must be the reactor containment chamber, for the warning signs adorning the small hatch leading inside. It's sealed, barred from the outside.

I pull aside the heavy lead shield obscuring the porthole-sized window.

Peering inside, a faint blue light emanates. His light. At the compartment's center sits a tall metal cylinder, the top half only—the rest of the shape is clearly embedded in the deck. The reactor. All manner of small pipes and hoses sprout from it. What looks to be a pump wheel. But the post is unmanned. Empty. I turn, looking to the hatch at the far end of the compartment, on the other side of the hulking, humming engine.

This will be the bottommost aft compartment.

Where I'll find Lazlo.

I waste no time.

Wheeling and swinging open the heavy hatch, a wave of reek assaults me.

Human effluence. Rancid fish oil and sick.

My eyes must adjust to the darkness. A few points of light here. Small grease wicks that seem to only accentuate the gloom.

I step in, and my eyes begin to adjust. Shapes move in that dimness. Figures begin stirring from the canvas hammocks that hang between the tall main seawater tanks. My feet are damp as I step deeper into the reeking, narrow, low, place.

The Forgotten.

Not boys but lean, starved young men who must have toiled back here, in these recesses, perhaps since even before I was fished out of the sea.

Shirtless. Ragged. Racks of ribs protruding like washboards. Gruesome and noisome, and hollow beings.

Faces I have forgotten completely until now. Names that

were almost lost to me.

Edwin, with his brown eyes, his fringe of gunny-sack colored hair. Yes, of course I remember Edwin. A Demi sent aft years ago. Grown up now. But still alive. Perhaps too tall to work in the reactor chamber.

Chamberlain, with the missing pinky finger on his left hand. He had such a rich, warm voice. Before it broke.

And here is Francis, who could not remember his vocal assignments, no matter how many times we practiced them.

Jarod, with his fringe of red hair that always seemed to grow back within days of shearing.

Their names, their faces swimming back into memory.

Some I do not recognize at all. Some that have been brought aboard only to serve in engineering. Not even Forgotten. Not known.

They look at me as though I'm the ghost. As though I'm the one only half-living. Dark, lifeless eyes peering out at me from sunken sockets. I move deeper into the compartment.

"L-Lazlo," I call out.

Some shrink back, as though they've never before heard a human voice.

And, finally, one small, skinny figure approaches. The others part, making a path for him. No, it can't be Lazlo. This boy is too frail. Too short.

But, yes, it is. By the light, I see the gleam in his eye … the familiar face, though starved and warped almost beyond comprehension.

And he smiles.

Lazlo.

Such brightness. Such light doesn't belong here, in this place. But it tells me that this ghost of a boy is, indeed, him.

My Lazlo.

I rush forward. Clutch him. Squeeze his body so tight, his bones press into me.

And he embraces me. Eventually. Carefully. Cautiously. And then fully, a grip so tight about my middle that my breath is almost taken from me.

I fight back the tears.

No time for that now.

"You received my message?" I ask, pulling away to look at him.

He nods, still bewildered. Still unbelieving. But he nods.

"Is it time?" Edwin asks, stepping forward. Yes, I remember his voice.

"It is! We're going to get out . . ." I whisper. "All of us. We have to act fast."

"I've prepared them," Lazlo says, nodding behind him. "We're ready to help."

What at first seemed a weak rabble of figures now has transformed. Those who can, stand beside Lazlo in resolution. Stand tall.

There's also a flurry of activity. Several of them have stepped into action, one moving a large canister, pulling out a concealed bundle. Another, moving aside bedding, searching.

"We've gathered a bit of food," Lazlo says.

"And a few tools—they might do for weapons," Francis says, taking out a hammer, a piece of lead pipe, and a thin, rusted strip of steel.

I almost want to cry. "You've all done . . . so well . . . okay—"

"Shhh!" someone says. "He's coming."

I look back to the hatchway, still hanging open.

"What's this . . ." Brother Dormer begins as he barges in, but halts. He sees the tools—the weapons—hanging in hands.

Sees me.

Before I can speak, before I can even move, one of the Forgotten has sprung on top of him, clawing. Another, striking out with his fists. Brother Dormer, caught off his guard, is knocked to the deck in a stupor, fending off the attack best he can with his arms out in front of him.

Others join.

Chamberlain and Jarod. And then Edwin, with what must be a sack of bolts in hand. He raises the bludgeon, ready to swing, but I clutch his arm before he can bring it down.

"*No!*" I say.

They are all looking at me. Fury and hatred. Pain, all pouring from their eyes.

"He isn't . . . he isn't bad," I say.

"They've starved us," Edwin says, voice raw. Cheeks wet. "They've *beaten* us . . ."

"We might need help from them in the end. Anyway, they're trapped too."

Brother Dormer stares up at me, a dumb, shocked expression.

"Trapped in a different sort of way," I continue. "That's why we're going to save as many of the brothers as we can. Is that clear?"

No one answers for a time. I worry that I've lost them—that they'll push me out.

"What's next?" Edwin finally asks, easing the tension.

"We have to shut down the engine and force the boat to surface," I say. "Shut down the hydraulics. The power. Can we do that?"

It's Lazlo who answers. "Yes."

Others in the circle nod in agreement.

"We need to seal off engineering completely."

"And then what? What are we waiting for?" Lazlo asks.

"A rescue."

"A rescue? From who?" Edwin asks.

"Topsiders . . ." I say.

Perhaps a few concerned or shocked expressions, but I receive no resistance. They all nod. They're ready.

It doesn't matter who it is rescuing them. Anything must be better than this.

"You'll need to take the maneuvering shack," I say. "Brother Leighton should be on duty."

"We can handle him," Edwin says.

"Before he can alert the bridge," I say. "Don't kill him."

They all nod in response. Lazlo.

"Okay. I'll be back."

"Wait—" Lazlo says, latching on to my arm like a vise. "Don't go. Not without me."

"There's a prisoner. Someone who has been helping me . . . helping us. She's important. I have to free her. . . ."

"Then you'll need at least two. I'll go with you," Edwin says.

"And me," Chamberlain agrees.

"No," I say. "It'll have to be me alone. Anyone else walking through will be too conspicuous."

A deep *thong* resounds throughout the boat. Hammer against hull.

Now is the hour for private prayer and reflection.

Now is the time to act.

"I have to go now," I say to all of them. "The chapel will be clear. Keep the hatch sealed until I return. I'll knock three times."

I ready myself, turn away, but Lazlo is still gripping my hand. Tears in his eyes.

I embrace him again. Deeply. He is weak. So weak, in fact, that it is me who is helping to brace him. "They have treatments Topside," I say. "They'll be able to help you."

His frail body quakes.

"I'll return," I say. "Soon."

I glance down at Brother Dormer as I go, now lying bound on the deck. Not struggling. Not fighting. He tracks me with his eyes as I pass. As though I am some alien creature.

———————

I pause at the hatchway to the chapel, peer inside.

Empty—just as I had hoped. The evening meal is soon to be served.

There, on the port side of the long chamber, on the other side of the missile tubes, a line of what were once former offices but are now used as cells. The third one is where Adolphine is being kept.

"It's me," I whisper through the vents at the top of the metal door, then unlatch it slowly.

With a grease wick in hand, I swing the door open, find a figure dressed in rags, huddled in the corner of the small compartment.

"Re-Remy?" a cautious voice asks, confused, blinking away the light, unfolding herself from her curled position cautiously. Here, now standing before me, Adolphine. A face I have only seen in profile. But a voice I know well. My confessor these past weeks.

She's a lean and sinewy woman. Her black, braided hair,

pulled back, featuring a gaunt face. Her eyes are the only thing familiar, other than her voice.

"We have to go forward with the plan . . . now," I whisper, glancing quickly at either end of the chapel hatchways and ladders. Still clear.

"But . . . but it's early," she says, understanding now what is happening. "We're a day early, isn't that right? We're not at the coordinates."

"There's no choice," I whisper. "No time to explain. We'll be caught if we don't act now. The Forgotten. They're taking control of engineering as we speak."

She blinks in response, stares forlornly at the deck. As though she is confused. Lost.

"You . . . you have the key with you?" she asks. Perhaps she didn't hear me. "The missile key?"

"Yes," I say, removing it from my robe pocket, holding it in my hand.

"Good," she says, oddly, looking at me—or, perhaps through me.

She's dazed. Hungry. Exhausted.

"Hurry now!" I turn to rush aft, but she doesn't follow. Instead, she has seized my wrist tight.

"What?" I ask as she pulls the key free from my hand.

In her expression, both fright and fury. "It's too soon," she whispers. "I haven't finished fixing the missile yet."

"That's good, isn't it? Come . . ." I try to pull her along, but she will not budge. She remains at the doorway of her cell.

My heart sinks, looking back at her, into her brown eyes.

"This is our only chance," she says. "Our last chance to take out the Liánméng fleet. They're all docked . . . in one place. If we act now, then it's over. The war will be over."

I try to pull away now, but she won't let me. She's gripping my arm so tightly, it burns.

Deep dread pours all over me. Seizes my bones. "I ... I thought you said ... you said there would be peace."

"There will be. I promise you that," she says. Her eyes darken.

"Liar ..." I whisper.

"I know, child," she says, patting my hand. "This was always our mission. One missile left in the world ... one last chance to end the war. We had to find the *Leviathan,* to make it operational again. To launch it. I could not have done it without you."

"Lazlo ... we were going to save him ... the others." I finally manage to pull away, but she seizes my shoulders, fingers digging in, yanks me close to her.

"You forget that boy, hear me?" she whispers now. "You can still save yourself ... slip away from them when we are at launch depth ... that will be no more than two hundred feet. You can ditch at that depth. Remember what I told you—"

"No," I say, breaking down, crying. Not believing it.

She, too, is crying. This stranger. She kisses my cheek. Now she has taken both my arms, gripping them tight. Not to embrace but to restrain me. To keep me from fleeing.

"*Save yourself,*" she whispers hotly into my ear. Then she shouts. "*Here!*" Louder than any voice has uttered on this boat. "He's trying to escape!"

8

I WAKE TO DIMNESS. Smell of rust, rancid oil. Vision blurry, a figure takes shape. I am on the deck, in Caplain's quarters, hands bound behind my back. Wrists at painful angles, numb.

Marston is seated at his desk, parchment laid out before him, three oil lamps lit, flames guttering.

He's humming an energetic tune.

I try to move. Can do little more than lift my head.

"I'm finishing our final hymn," he says, without turning or looking. He must have heard me stir. "What we shall sing as we descend. The final song we shall sing into the deep."

He turns in his chair. About his neck hangs the missile key. The real one. In his hands, folded sheaves of parchment. He blows on the ink to dry it, then shows me the cover of the folio. Penned there, in ornamental lettering, the words *Cantio Maris.*
Song of the Sea.

"I've known you can read for some time—Latin as well," he says, setting the folio on the desk behind him. Then he leans in close. "I know many of the secrets you and Caplain Amita shared. But the big one—I only just sussed that out a few years ago."

"You knew?" I lick my lips. An arc of fire. I taste dried blood.

"He didn't tell me—Caplain Amita. I figured it out on my own. I heard it in your voice, eventually. There's a . . . unique quality to the castrati voice. Beautiful, yes. But a shade away from natural. Not yours, though."

"And why have you kept me alive, then? So long after Caplain Amita's death."

"Because of your voice, child. Faith needs nurturing . . . our little flame, here in the darkness, in need of stoking," he says, peering up, to an unknown height. "You have lifted us up for so long. That is why Caplain kept your secret, no doubt. He knew your . . . utility.

"My, my, but you have kept your own confidences and kept them well." He looks down at the key hanging about his neck. "This, I did not know about. That Amita had kept the real key hidden all this time. That he gave the real one to you."

"He didn't trust you . . ." I say, throat dry.

"He was the one not to be trusted, Remy," Marston says, standing now. So very tall from this position. Crooked. "He knew all along the missile would not fire. He had no intention of delivering the Last Judgment."

"There is a world out there . . ."

"Sinners."

"People. Good people . . ."

"People like this woman. Adolphine. She who lied to you, who took advantage of you to serve her own whims? She's told me everything. About your plan for escape, for rescue. The message you sent." He shakes his head.

"What happened to her?"

"You care? After all she has done? After her betrayal?"

Survive, she whispered to me.

"I do," I say.

"She finished repairing the Last Judgment. Then she was returned to the sea. Where she belongs. God will decide the fate of her soul. Whether she redeemed herself."

I close my eyes.

"She reprogrammed the missile," I say. "It won't strike where you want it to. It isn't even targeted at Sydney any longer. Without her, you won't be able to reprogram it."

Marston laughs gently to himself, oddly.

"You think it matters where the missile strikes? It is the last. Blessed by God. It will usher in the end of days regardless."

These words. I once believed them. How, now, is it that they sound so unfamiliar?

"There will be no rescue, dear Remy," he says with a mock sympathy. "Even the closest Coalition ships are days away. And the Liánméng submarine that attacked has not followed us into these waters."

I fight the urge to cry, even though a heat is building. A stinging.

"I see in you the same weakness as our beloved Caplain," Marston says, staring down at me fixedly. Disappointed. "The same I saw in Brother Calvert's eyes. Yes, I know he was the one who turned on us. Divulged the secrets of our order to the Topsiders. Oh, how you've been seduced ... how easily, by his lies. The lies of your friend, Adolphine. You were ready to leave us ... to abandon our order, after we have given you everything."

"You've starved us ... beaten us ... mutilated us. Lied to us," I say. I know now these are words I've wanted to speak out loud, to utter, for longer than I even knew.

"To try and purify you ... but I can see that has not worked. Not for you or for Lazlo."

"Caplain Amita gave me the key for a reason," I say. "He wanted me ... me to decide. To be able to say that no ... the time is not right. Perhaps it would never be right. He knew that."

"And he was a fool who had lost his faith in the end. Thank God I am here to enact His plan for the world. And we must ready ourselves," Marston says, nodding, reveling in his own righteousness. "Your heart is corrupted, but you are too important to be rid of here . . . in these final hours."

"Utility," I say.

He nods.

"You should ask St. John to sing your hymn. He is very eager."

Caplain Marston gives a short, dry laugh. "He is that. But even if he was in a place to sing, after you unleashed your . . . fury upon him, he does not have your gift. No, I wrote this for you."

"But why would I sing now?" I say, trying to sit up. "Sing for you?"

"Not for me . . . for your brothers. For Lazlo. Don't you want to give them some comfort before we descend . . . an exaltation of the spirit?"

I don't answer.

He frowns.

"Sing the Cantio," he says, "and I will let you see Lazlo again. I will bring him back from Engineering. You will spend your last hours with him."

I search Marston's face for sincerity. Indeed, he has said these words with the same intense conviction in which he has said everything else.

Lazlo. If he is with me, then perhaps we could still flee together. Find a way to escape. Like Adolphine said.

"But . . . I don't believe anymore," I say, honest as I can. Strong as I can. "I don't know if I ever really did."

"Ah, but you don't have to *believe* in order to be a vessel for the Holy Spirit. Your dear Adolphine is proof of that. Look what she did for us—repaired the Last Judgment. Like Solomon, like Paul—a tool of God."

He believes it. Everything he is saying, he believes.

"And when you were done with her, you killed her," I say.

"We could not have an interloper on board during our final hours."

"But you'll have a woman aboard," I say. "You haven't told them, have you? The brothers? They don't know."

Marston pauses. Stands straighter. I've caught him out. The only time I've seen him flinch. "No," he says, steely.

"All the lies you've built this place upon . . . you and Caplain Amita both—you know that if they knew about me, it would cause people to doubt. That I was conspiring with a Topsider, that I was going to escape." The words keep coming. They won't stop. "St. John knows. I saw the confusion when he discovered my secret."

Marston bends down, pinches my chin, tight. Leans in. I couldn't turn away from his narrow, yellowed face if I wanted. "St. John knows how important our mission is. He'll be dutiful to the order. And if you will not—if you attempt to say a word—then I will take Lazlo's life with my own hands. While you watch. I promise you that."

Beady eyes, dark. Almost dead with resolve.

I swallow. My throat, thick.

Agreeing means that I will be let free. Agreeing means that Lazlo will be with me and that we still might possibly find a way out.

I nod once, silently.

"Tomorrow, then," he says, releasing his grip, standing straight, smoothing out his robes. "Tomorrow will be our grand day. Our salvation. I suggest you pray, dear Remy. Pray that you might be forgiven your trespasses. He might just listen."

———————

The deck had been at an upward tilt. Now it levels.

The hammer throngs against the hull. Three resonant blows.

Call to Compline.

The final office in the liturgy of the hours.

We brothers were often asked, in this hour, to contemplate our actions and thoughts in the day. An examination of conscience.

This was common when Caplain Amita was still alive.

Have our actions and thoughts aligned with our moral code? The order by which we have all promised to live our lives?

Sometimes, I felt I had strayed. My thoughts had often bent toward those scant memories of my life Topside. Of sunlight. Of bright-tasting limes. Even though I knew I should not let them stray. To dwell on such memories was the same as wishing to live amongst the Forsaken. Amongst the sinners.

I often thought that my very existence was an aberration.

Me, a woman. A forbidden figure amongst the penitent men, living a lie.

Caplain Amita tried to assuage this guilt when I confessed it to him.

"You are doing God's work," he would say. *"A vessel for God. And God will watch after you."*

But this was the same argument Marston gave.

Utility.

It does not matter what you think, what you feel, how you act, so long as it is God's work.

An ultimate hypocrisy—this from the man I thought had taken care of me for so long. The man I thought loved me. The one who started all this—who helped to end the world, who tossed little girls screaming into the sea, and took the boys and cut them so that they might remain eternally pure.

I look at my hands, in the dimness of the officers' quarters I have been locked in for the past day. Wash them in the bowl of rare fresh water brought to me in a chipped clay bowl. Splash my face. Taste the salty grit trickling down over my lips. I pull on clean, newly sewn robes. Marston has given me fresh linen strips for binding my chest. These, I don't wear. If I am to die, I will go to God the way I was put into the world.

When the rusted, squealing latch is finally pulled aside, I stand. The door swings open, and a blazing amber, putrid light pours in. Every lamp and grease wick ablaze. Ex-Oh Goines and Brother Augustine await me to exit, and then escort me, standing on either side, to the chapel, down to the lower deck, past the radio room, which is empty, past the missile control room, which is manned by Brothers Elia and Cordova, both seated before a wide bank of electronic panels that are already lit up. They watch as I pass.

I am pushed forward, ducking through the hatch, and stand to find almost all the brothers lining the walls of the chapel, staggered between, around, and behind the missile tubes. All bow their heads in silence as I pass.

Brother Ernesto. Ignacio. Andrew. Callum. Jessup. Pike.

Do some of them know the truth? That I was conspiring with a Topsider? That I was planning on escaping? Brother

Callum might. He knows this is madness. He might not have the words to express it, but he knows. I saw it the night I dosed his steep with the nostrum, when he recounted his story of first being brought aboard.

But he will not look at me. No, he will not act.

He will be complicit in all of this.

At the end of the long compartment, atop the driftwood dais, Captain Marston stands, eyeing me intently.

And, before the dais, before the psalter, Ephraim. Mouth drawn tight, eyes weighted. St. John, face swollen, welted red and purple from my attack. He is staring directly at me. Yet I don't find fury or contempt there, as I would expect after what I did to him. Not even coldness. It's a vacancy.

And there, beside them all, Lazlo.

He, too, is looking directly at me, but his eyes are still very full of light.

Lazlo.

Did he, for a moment, dare to dream that there might be an escape for us?

There still might be.

If I could slip away. Take Lazlo with me. Marston said the Coalition ships might be an ocean away, but they also might be closer than that. It would only mean surviving a day or two on the open seas if they are indeed on their way to the rendezvous.

If.

Too many ifs.

The reality of it begins to drape over me.

A coldness.

That this is it.

I see now that both the hatchways at either end of the compartment are being guarded. The ladders down to the lower level. There's no escape.

This is my fate. Our fate.

As I take my place beside Lazlo, St. John, and Ephraim, the brothers turn their attention to Marston, who, tall and energized, opens with the psalm.

"*Ecce nunc benedicite Dominum.*"

And then the Canticle of Simeon.

"*Nunc dimittis servum tuum, Domine, secundum verbum tuum in pace: Quia viderunt oculi mei salutare tuum.*"

Lord, now lettest Thou Thy servant depart in peace according to Thy word.

For mine eyes have seen Thy salvation.

I have no voice for the chant. No spirit. No, the light is robbed from me. Drained. What was once a freedom feels like the greatest, the weightiest of shackles.

I glance to Lazlo, standing just beside me.

His fingers find mine. Cold and thin. I entwine mine with his.

We don't care who sees.

"My brothers, we are soon to launch the Last Judgment," Marston says solemnly, with great dramatic effect, after the calls and the responses are complete. "When we do, we shall finish what was started some twenty-four years ago. And we shall dive to the deepest depth. We shall sing a song into that deep—a hymn I have heard in that darkness—the Lord has whispered unto me the words that will ready our souls for His glory!"

Before us, the psalter is opened.

Cantio Maris.

I see penned on the top stave of each page the descant that is meant for me. Just looking at it, I can hear the melody in my mind. Something exalting. Stilted.

What darkness we have lighted, one of the lyrics reads. *They above shall know what we below have sent.*

"Yes, we shall know salvation," Marston continues. "Salvation, after these years of service. Of maintaining the order begun by our beloved Caplain Amita. We shall see him again, brothers. We shall see so many faces that we have long ago committed to the sea. And the sea shall give up her dead," he says, eyes lit with a fervor, a passion.

"And the sea shall give up her dead!" the brothers respond.

"As below, so above," Caplain says.

And the congregation answers.

When I glance upward, Marston is staring down to me. The others are watching as well. Expectantly.

Now is my time.

Here is my purpose. The very reason I was saved, eight years ago. The only reason.

I am to sing now.

In my brothers' eyes, I am holy. Special. Caplain Amita has told me this all along. Fed me this lie.

But should I not ease their worry? Lighten their souls? If we are all to die. To sink down and down until, at last, the depths crush us.

And so, I sing.

I open my mouth, find my voice. Find an energy that was not there before.

But I do not sing Marston's hymn.

I sing my own Song of the Sea. A song the leviathans have taught me. No words. Just melody. An odd, sorrowful strain that leaps and dives in pitch, that slides into bitter notes and then resolves.

I close my eyes while I sing. Let the melody take its own form. Like when I have sung during Terce. Improvisation. But more than that. I think of that one whale, searching for the other. Its lover, its friend, its child. Whatever it is. It's a song that seeks out. That searches. That mourns. That hopes.

And when I have finished the song and open my eyes, I find the chapel utterly silent. And yet, I feel the weight of all sixty-seven pairs of eyes upon me, can almost hear sixty-seven hearts thrumming in some kind of unity.

Then I glance up to Caplain Marston. Gaze narrowed, piercing. Face tight with fury.

"It's time, my brothers," he finally says, hollowly, shattering the silence. "Watch, are we at depth?"

"Ready, Caplain. We need only finish bringing the targeting computer online," Brother Marcus says.

"Good. Cantor Remy," Marston says through gritted teeth. "You will follow me."

St. John flicks a quick glance my way. Ephraim.

Where is he taking me?

Is this punishment for my betrayal?

I glance around at the room, at the faces of my fellow Choristers, the brothers, all watching, eyes twinkling in amber light. Faces bent in some emotion I cannot read. Cheeks wet.

I release Lazlo's hand. I must. No other choice. I try telling him everything I want to with just a look, should this be the last time I ever see him.

Marston commands St. John lead the brothers in the singing of the final hymn, and then I'm immediately led back through the center of the chapel, between brothers and the column-like missile tubes, back through the hatch, to the missile control room.

The small space is hot with the humming equipment, with the several bodies crammed inside.

Six of us with Elia and Cordova, and Ex-Oh Goines and Brother Augustine, both of whom will not leave my side, and Caplain Marston.

On the main panel, two rows of square indicators, eight in each, each numbered, are lit. Fifteen of them glow red. One of them glows green. The Last Judgment.

"Missile is ready for launch, Caplain," Brother Cordova says. Before him, on the desk console, the red CAPTAIN indicator switches to green. Beneath this indicator is a round, metal slot for the missile key.

Ex-Oh grabs hold of my arms from behind, grip tight.

Caplain Marston turns to me. "I wanted you to see this, Cantor. To understand that God's will cannot be undermined. Cannot be changed."

I glance at the others, at Brother Augustine. He shares a tense expression.

From the chapel, I hear the hymn being sung now. "The Heart of the Leviathan."

"And the sinners shall know fire once more."

"Tube pressurized, Caplain," a crackling voice calls from the squawk box. *"Missile door open. Ready to fire."*

I watch as Marston feeds the stem of the key into the slot, as he turns it.

The launch indicator for Missile 1 flashes.

A siren chimes throughout the boat.

The singing has ceased in the chapel. Silence now, save the normal thrumming of engines and fans and the hiss of stale, oily air from the vent.

Caplain's eyes are closed, in prayer, finger hovering over the plastic button marked "Launch."

I couldn't stop him if I wanted to, not with Ex-Oh holding my arms back.

Will the world end?

It already has. Been ended and then reborn. Were we ever on the edge of peace? No, I think not. Not now. Not ever.

Maybe the world will never be saved.

"*Woe! Woe to you, great city, you mighty city of Babylon!*" Caplain Marston begins. His voice is being amplified throughout the boat, over the squawk.

Won't anyone step up and stop this? Anyone? I look to the old, weary elders. To Brothers Carrington and Goines. Neither will Brother Dormer or Augustine or Callum. No. They haven't stepped in before now. During all the horrors and atrocities that have occurred these long years. None of them tried to stop it.

So, I pray.

"*The seventh angel poured out his bowl into the air, and a loud voice came out of the temple, from the throne, saying, 'It is done!'*"

I pray that the electricity will wink out. That the ballast mains will burst. That the Liánméng will attack us.

"*And there were flashes of lightning, rumblings, peals of thunder, and a great earthquake such as there had never been since man was on the earth.*"

The pipes continue to pressurize in the underworks. I hear the high-pitched whine.

"*The cities of the nations fell, and God remembered Babylon the great, to make her drain the cup of the wine of the fury of his wrath.*"

I pray that the blue, hot reactor will suddenly blow, will end all this right now.

"*And every island fled away, and no mountains were to be found. And the Lord rose up, with the wicked stricken from this place, forever, finally finding a purified kingdom of heaven on earth.*"

Please!

"*As below, so above!*"

And then the cabin goes dark.

Just like that.

The main lights die, as do the consoles, the missile control. Auxiliary lights flash on.

Yellow lights spin now.

Warning lights for contamination.

This is no attack by the Topsiders.

The reactor.

"*Caplain,*" a crackling voice cries out over the squawk box, "*Reactor coolant line just failed—it's overhea—*"

The rest of the transmission is cut short by a thunderous resonance emanating from aft. From engineering. A shudder through the very vessel. Then a roar.

A wave of heat and toxic fume wash through the cabin, through the chapel.

"Stations!" Caplain Marston shouts. The men in the room scramble.

Looking through the hatch, to the far side of the chapel, I see the glow of red flame. In the chapel, a mass of rushing shadows and shapes. Lazlo is among them, but I can't see him—I am hooked about the shoulder by a powerful, cinching grip. Marston has ensnared me with his long reach.

"What have you done?" he demands, long face before mine. Long hands grappling my neck.

"Nothing . . ." I try to say, but the words are choked from me.

"You were sent by Satan, weren't you?" he says, eyes blazing, face bent into a sneer. "Sent to ruin us. To thwart God's will!"

I can't breathe—can't even gasp for the tightness.

Another pronounced bang causes the entire vessel to shiver. Then the world suddenly tilts, pitches downward. The caplain releases his grip, is knocked off his balance, falls, slides down nearly the full length of the corridor.

I catch myself on the entryway to missile control. Many other brothers tumble past me, scrambling for a grip. Brother Andrew. Brother Ernesto. Marcus.

"Dive planes aren't responding!" a voice calls out over the squawk.

The *Leviathan* cants severely to starboard. One of the trim tanks has failed.

We're going down.

I begin scaling up the inclined corridor, gripping the bulkhead in order to pull myself through the hatchway into the chapel, which is a riot of shouting, a smoke-filled and dim chaos.

"Lazlo!" I call out.

Brother Callum swims into view, clinging to one of the missile tube hatches. "Brace yourself . . . we're going . . ."

He is slammed suddenly into the bulkhead as the whole boat lurches, screeches. A deafening report of clashing metal.

Impact.

My grip is shaken from me. I'm knocked to the deck.

The *Leviathan* has struck bottom. Heavy. Hard. The Arafura Sea is shallow, though. Just like Adolphine said, we can't be more than forty fathoms deep.

Now comes the unmistakable hiss of ruptured pipes followed by a roaring torrent coming from deck below. The hull has been breached.

The klaxon blares.

The hatch to engineering is closed, sealed. The only entry to the tunnel. The fate of the Forgotten is now sealed. How many souls will be lost?

The deck has leveled. I push through the smoke, the confusion, past faceless, lurking, coughing forms. Brother Peter? Brother Jenner? I stumble over a fallen figure. I cannot see who, only that the shape is too big to be Lazlo.

Finally, I see a familiar figure in the flashing yellow lights. Ephraim. He is bracing a small, thin shadowed person.

"Lazlo!" I embrace him, his thin, emaciated body, so tight, I feel the breath go out of him. I feel his arms close around me.

"Come on," I say, pulling both him and Ephraim along, forward.

"Where can we go?" he asks, coughing.

"We're going to ditch," I say.

The escape trunk at the top of the balneary. That's the only way off this ship. The only way to survive.

We've pushed through the crowd, past Brother Alban, Brother Henry, bent over, kneeling, praying.

"Come on!" I shout to them. "Come follow us!"

But they do not.

Behind us, a wrenching burst. A watery roar.

The bulkhead to engineering has breached.

Two of the missile tube access ports have blown at the far end of the compartment. Frothing, boiling water floods, washing away the wooden dais. Electronics sparking, components hissing angry steam.

"Hold on!" I say, anchoring myself and Lazlo against one of

the missile tubes. Ephraim does the same. When the first rush of seawater gushes forward, it almost sweeps us away.

But this is the direction we must go. And fast.

"Come!" I shout, letting go my handhold, trying not to be sucked through the hatch. Bracing the edges of the entryway, I duck through, then swing around to catch Lazlo as he shoots in. Then Ephraim.

"We should seal the compartment!" Ephraim shouts.

But the force of the water is too great. I've lost my grip. The jetting current carries us down the corridor, past mission control, past the radio room, into the mess hall, where flailing bodies and debris have been pushed by the current. The hatchway to the balneary is just ahead, through the chaos of screams and choking and coughing. The water is up to our waists and rising.

I look back to find Lazlo still behind me, and Ephraim.

Lazlo's hand is thin, slippery in the cold water, but still I pull him along, not letting go, grabbing pipes, cables, anything along the ceiling to grab to keep our heads above the fast-rising water.

"Follow us," I shout, seeing Brother Dumas's face in the near darkness. "A way out."

But he doesn't seem to hear. He is swimming aft, in the opposite direction, toward the ladder to the upper deck.

The *Leviathan* groans, squeals. A fresh influx of water tells me there's been another hull breach.

We're almost to the balneary hatchway when I hear Lazlo shriek behind me.

I spin around to find that he's being pulled under, being pulled back. I struggle to keep my grip on his hand. It's Marston, face bloodied. He's latched onto Lazlo, is forcing his head beneath the water.

"I told you what I would do!" the old man spits, his chin only just above the rising, frothing seawater.

I fling myself at him, the tall man, trying to pull at his arm, grappling, scratching. But his grip is strong and his reach so long. He is both able to hold Lazlo under and keep me at a distance.

"Let him go!" I hear Ephraim shout. He's tackled the caplain as well, has wrapped his arms around the older man's neck.

This has surprised Marston. He loosens his grip. Lazlo surfaces, sputtering, gasping, blinded by the salty water. I reach out, pull him away from the caplain's reach, push him through the hatchway to the balneary.

I see Ephraim still struggling with Marston, unable to overtake the man. The caplain is able to keep his nose and mouth just above the surface of the water, while Ephraim is not.

"Let him go!" I shout, about to swim into the fray once more when a sound like the tolling of the hammer against the hull but louder, deeper, rings out. The water level suddenly recedes. The *Leviathan*'s position on the sea floor must be shifting, sliding. Marston and Ephraim are swept backward, downward. I cling to a pipe on the ceiling and reach out. Ephraim reaches for me but does not find my hand before he is sucked away.

The lights go completely out now. Batteries blown. Total darkness.

Chaos. Cacophony and darkness.

"Remy!" Lazlo calls out.

"Here," I say, turning. If we're going to survive, we have to leave now. I know it.

I hate it, but I know it.

The water level, momentarily lowered, is rising again, the

torrent of cold seawater still spilling in through the breaches on this level, and now from above.

Into the balneary. I see two bodies floating, both facedown in the water. Both with shorn heads. Matching robes. They could be anyone. Any of the brothers.

Something else is floating in the rising water. The inflatable life raft from the *Janus*. New life vests, also pillaged from Adolphine's ship.

"Climb!" I say, forcing Lazlo up the ladder first, into the open hatch of the escape trunk. I follow behind him with the uninflated life raft in hand, seal the hatch behind me.

Inside the tight compartment, an auxiliary light still glows. Casts us both in lurid red.

I think back to the lessons that Brother Calvert taught me—how to escape. How to equalize the pressure in the hatch in order to make the water level rise to the level of the escape hatch at the top of the compartment.

I turn the red valve that controls the pressure. There's a hissing, and water begins flooding the compartment.

"Remy!" Lazlo says, fearful.

"We have to flood the chamber if we want to escape," I say, trying to calm him.

All the while, the boat continues to shift beneath us, groans, pops, hisses—the water line tilts.

"I . . . I can't swim," he says, gasping.

"Neither can I. Here," I say, fitting a life vest over his head, fastening it around his middle before securing my own. "Remember what Brother Calvert told us. These will keep us afloat. These will send us to the surface. We'll shoot right up!"

He stares at the rising water, breathing fast.

"Just remember to blow out . . ." I say, panting myself. "Blow out all the way up. You'll have more than enough air in your lungs."

He isn't hearing me. Isn't hearing anything, his eyes hollow and pale, shaking. In shock.

"It's time," I say, taking his face in both my hands, forcing him to acknowledge my words.

He nods once. I shut off the valve just after the rising water clears the hood for the hatch, leaving us a small pocket of air remaining at the very top of the compartment. Then I duck under and open the hatch, which swings down on its hinge. "Okay, you first," I say after surfacing, wiping the water from my eyes.

The boat groans, tilts even more to the port. The pocket of air shrinks.

"*Now!*" I say.

He takes a deep breath, then disappears beneath the hatch hood.

I follow, first grabbing the life raft, then ducking under and out.

I'm shooting up, rocketing through the water, blowing out the air in my lungs, even though that seems like the most un-natural thing to do.

But my lungs do not deflate—no, there is more than enough to expel and still be full. The oddest feeling.

Up and up—my eyes burn from the water, but I keep them open, looking down, beneath me—this ocean is nowhere near as black as I imagined—I see the dim shapes, retreating in the darkness—the *Leviathan*—the massive black vessel, bleeding bubbles—and what must be the mis-sile—the Last Judgment, its white shell seeming to glow in the dimness, expelled from its missile tube upon impact. It did not launch. It did not reach the surface.

I finally must close my eyes from the stinging, but even behind my eyelids, head now tilted upward, I see a light. A growing brightness. The water grows warmer on my skin. My ears pop—it feels as though my head may burst from the pressure, but, finally, finally, I breach the surface, splash into open air and open my eyes to daylight—the brightest light I have ever seen. My eyes, utterly blinded by it.

It should be night, I realize.

We had only just finished with Compline, the night prayer. But up here, it is day.

I cough. Suck in a breath of clean air.

A rush of wind upon my head, my cheeks.

Finally, after I blink away the burning, my eyes take it in—a blue sea, a clear sky, a sun resting halfway to the distant, distant line that must be the horizon.

"Lazlo!" I call out.

And I hear a weak answer.

Some twenty feet away, he bobs, gagging, panicking, thrashing in the water.

Paddling to him, I embrace him again, and he clings onto my arm.

I pull the release valve on the bundle still clutched in my hand. With a sudden burst and hiss, the raft inflates, exploding from the size of a small flat box to a vessel large enough to fit ten at least.

Another violent splashing behind us.

I turn to see a shape emerge from the sudden geyser of bubbles—a figure, bursting to the surface, choking.

Edwin. He is clinging to an empty jug.

At least one of the Forgotten has survived.

"Here!" I shout out. "Edwin!" I realize that he can't see me. He's still blinded by the sunlight.

He paddles frantically, squinting. "Remy?"

"Here!"

Another splash. It's Jarod, also from engineering.

And another—a face I saw for the first time upon journeying into engineering. A tall, thin young man whose name I don't know.

"How ever did you escape?" I ask.

"We were locked in our berthing, but that second explosion warped the door. Made it out the rear trunk," Edwin says, coughing.

I turn in the water to see a shape emerge from another geyser of bubbles.

Ephraim.

He's clinging to a net float. Blinking, stunned, like all of us—looking upon this vast, bright world the way I imagine a newborn babe would.

"Ephraim," I shout, reaching for him. He finds my hand, and I pull him closer to the raft. "You made it."

"St. John—" he says, hacking, spitting up water. "He guided me out. Through the breached missile tube."

Another violent splashing behind us.

St. John. His pate split and bleeding. He spins, thrashes in the water, among the growing slick of oil and fuel, the flotsam of the wreck of the *Leviathan*, clinging to an empty water tank for buoyancy.

"Here," I call out.

And he turns, still squinting. A curtain of blood spilling into his eyes.

"Here," I say again.

He finally spots us, splashes over, grips hold of the lines edging the life raft and pulls himself up and inside in one go.

I fear, for a moment, that he might leave us here. Maybe he considers it to. But if so, it's only for a moment. He helps me to get Lazlo into the raft, pulling him up by the tops of his life jacket.

And then he helps to heave me aboard. Ephraim. Together, we help with Edwin and Jarod.

After, we all gasp, breathing, sitting in silence in the raft, looking around us, at the cloudless sky, at the blue, blue sea.

We wait, amidst the churning water, for others to rise.

They do not.

9

THE GREAT SILENCE COMES when darkness fully falls. The hours that follow Compline. No speaking, of course. But also a time where every action should be made softly. Every movement. Every footstep. A time for rest, for prayer.

I have no will in me for either.

We have been spit from the belly of the beast. Not safely upon a shore, but alive. Seven of us. For a time.

I must have done God's will, in the end. The missile did not launch. It was thwarted. By divine intervention?

Something inside stops me from believing that, reminds me of how dangerous it is to believe that.

Little waves lap at the gunwales of the rubber raft, slap beneath us. They are not large. Do no more than rock us lightly, roll beneath. Night has almost fallen, and we all gaze above at the cloudless expanse of deepening sky, a bowl already blue and sprinkled with what must be stars. For I do not remember stars. Have only read about them.

The way the ancients once navigated, finding patterns and trustworthiness in their constant positions.

My mind doesn't know what to do with it—this expanse of sky—these endless reaches. It feels as though I'm looking down instead of up, into a wholly different sea, about to fall in.

I must close my eyes.

Lazlo shivers in my arms.

His thin body, a collection of sharp bones kept contained in bible-paper thin skin.

The stars offer light enough to see his scrubby head mottled with sores, his angled cheekbones.

"I did right," he whispers softly.

"What?"

"I did right. I broke the reactor," he says. His voice is little. It's weak. "I loosened a coupler on the pressure line. I knew I had to do something . . . knew you must have been captured. The others . . . they helped, too."

Edwin is still awake, sitting up, watching in silence.

Lazlo coughs. A wet sound.

I look down to find glossy black sputum on my arm.

"Yes," I whisper. "You did good. You saved us. You might have saved the world. What's left of it."

When I open my eyes again, it is fully night. Deep night. Stars blazing.

Something in my body tells me that it is time to rise and sing. Matins.

Time to praise the Lord, the very act of creation. Goodness and light.

And, as though answering, a faint, ever-so-soft crying fills the air. It's coming from under us. From beneath the waves.

A sorrowful bellow.

And then, an answer.

A sonorous, distant response. They are together again. The two whales. The ones that have been apart for so long.

"Listen," I whisper to Lazlo.

He does not answer.

I feel his full weight on me. I lean in to him, listening for the soft hiss of breath. Find it. Alive.

Only just.

St. John is still awake. Watching us from the other side of the raft. I see his bruised face by the starlight, his gleaming eyes.

"Does he know?" he asks. "The truth about you."

"No," I say, wiping my salt-chapped cheeks. "It won't matter to him, though."

This, I believe with all my heart. This, I have faith in.

Sometime later, St. John begins singing. It's a broken song, uttered by a broken voice.

The Benedictus.

Sung at Lauds, at the break of day.

"*Per viscera misericordiae Dei nostri, in quibus visitabit nos oriens ex alto,*" he sings.

In the tender compassion of our God the dawn from on high shall break upon us.

I join in with him. I'm not sure why. "*Illuminare his, qui in tenebris et in umbra mortis sedent.*"

To shine on those who dwell in darkness and the shadow of death.

Those of us who were former Choristers join in now. One last chorus. Our audience, the sea and sky. Lazlo stirs.

"There," St. John says suddenly, pointing to the horizon, sitting up, waking the others.

Just at the pale orange line that must be the coming dawn, a small shadow crosses. And then a flashing light. A ship.

In the raft, there is a kit. A bag labeled EMERGENCY FLARES. We can use them to signal this ship, whether it be friend or foe.

If that distinction matters.

St. John points one of the canisters to the sky, pulling the string at the end. The first does nothing. Neither do the following two. Duds. But the last one works. It spits a hot, brilliant, flaming bulb high into the sky. An arc of light that seems to take forever to finally fizzle and sink.

Whether the ship sees us, we cannot know.

So, we wait. Listening in great silence to the wind, to the lapping waves. To the leviathans.

They move unseen, beneath us, in that vast darkness. Singing, calling out to one another, answering. Exalting nothing, or perhaps everything. Every mountain and trench and cavern and creature in the sea. Every soul lost to it, waiting there, for the inkling of light to finally come.

Acknowledgments

My deepest thanks go out to Diana M. Pho, who acquired this novella, and to Lee Harris and the rest of the Tordotcom team for carrying it over the finish line. Additional thanks go to my agent, John Silbersack, and to Nicole Budrovich, for her linguistic expertise. I'm also grateful to Alicia Upano, Tony Bonds, and Robert Penner for their keen critical insights. Finally, thanks to Mary Stewart, ever my first reader.

About the Author

ANDREW KELLY STEWART's writing spans the literary, science fiction, fantasy, and supernatural genres. His short fiction has appeared in *The Magazine of Fantasy & Science Fiction* and *ZYZZYVA*. He is a Clarion Workshop alum and holds an MFA in creative writing. This is his first publication with Tordotcom Publishing. Stewart lives and writes in Southern California.

Twitter: @MrAndySt
andrewkellystewart.com

TOR·COM

Science fiction. Fantasy. The universe.

And related subjects.

*

More than just a publisher's website, *Tor.com* is a venue for **original fiction, comics,** and **discussion** of the entire field of SF and fantasy, in all media and from all sources. Visit our site today—and join the conversation yourself.